A Book of Mermaids

A BOOK OF
MERMAIDS

Ruth Manning-Sanders

Cover illustration by Mari Paige Hellman
Interior illustrations by Stephanie Vanicek
Typesetting by Claire Zimowski

MAB Media   Houston

by Ruth Manning-Sanders

A Book of Giants
A Book of Dwarfs
A Book of Dragons
A Book of Witches
A Book of Wizards
A Book of Mermaids

First published in the U.S.A., 1968, by E.P. Dutton & Co., Inc.
Reprinted 2016 by MAB Media
Copyright © 1967 by Ruth Manning-Sanders
All rights reserved. Printed in the U.S.A.

Library of Congress Control Number: 2016903170

A Book of Mermaids

by Ruth Manning-Sanders

Stories about mermaids come from almost every country by the sea—from Iceland to India; America to Arabia. Most mermaids have flowing golden hair, long graceful tails, and a beauty that lures men to the bottom of the sea. Sven, in the Danish story, "Sven and Lilli," followed Lilli to her ocean home, where "they live happily. And there, in their domed house under the sea, so people say, they are living still."

But not all mermaids are beautiful, and some are unchancy creatures indeed. There is a mermaid in the Irish tale, "The Magic Lake," who has "pig's eyes and wolf's teeth, and a mouth...grinning from ear to ear." And the beautiful mermaid Groach, in the Breton story, "The Groach of the Isle of Lok," casts a spell over handsome young men, marries them, and then turns them into rainbow-colored fish.

In these sixteen stories Ruth Manning-Sanders captures, with the true storyteller's relish of detail, the quicksilver personalities of mermaids and mermen and recounts with enthusiasm their marvelous schemes and adventures.

Contents

Foreword

I discovered *A Book of Mermaids* one hot summer day in our tiny, public library.

The magical people and places in Ruth Manning-Sanders' stories cemented my life-long love affair with books.

I am grateful to the estate of Ruth Manning-Sanders and her grandson John Floyd for giving me permission to reprint *A Book of Mermaids*.

Thanks to my family and friends who supported this endeavor, especially Claire Zimowski and Paige Hellman. You are stars!

Finally, I would also like to give a special "merci" to Fabrice for all his love and guidance.

I hope you enjoy these stories as much as I continue to do.

Best wishes and happy reading,

Melissa Buron
Publisher
MAB Media

Introduction

If you were asked to make a picture of a mermaid, you might possibly draw her with a comb in one hand and a looking glass in the other; but whether you gave her a comb and glass or not, you would certainly give her a tail. Because that is the way we all of us picture mermaids to be—beautiful creatures who sit on the rocks, comb their glittering hair and sing: creatures who are like human beings in every respect, except that instead of legs they have tails.

And so it may surprise you to learn that though many mermaids have tails and no legs, some have legs and no tail, and some have both legs and tails.

You will find tailless mermaids in the Breton story, *The Groach of the Isle of Lok,* and in the Welsh story, *The Lake Maiden,* where the mermaid walks on the water and wears golden sandals.

However, there do seem to be more mermaids with tails than without them, and there are plenty of tailed mermaids (and mermen) swimming about in these stories, which, as we should expect, come mostly from countries with a long seaboard. There are two stories from Ireland, *The Magical Tune,* and *The Magic Lake*; two from Scotland, *Merman Rosmer,* and *The Untidy Mermaid. The Lost Prince* comes from Iceland; *Rake Up!* from Denmark; *The Geese and the Golden Chain* from Portugal; *The Three Mermaids* from Italy; *The Kingdom of Ocean* from India; *The Comb, the Flute and the Spinning Wheel* from the north of Germany; and *Long John and the Mermaid* from America.

And what are they like, these mermen and mermaids, not in looks but in character? On the whole, they are unchancy creatures, particularly the mermaids. You can't trust a mermaid even as far as you can see her. For they have a habit of falling in love with handsome young men, and dragging them down under the water. Woe betide you, too, if you offend one of these sea people; for then they will raise such a storm of wind and wave that if you escape with your life, you are lucky.

Of course there are exceptions. In the Danish story, *Sven and Lilli*, the little mermaid is most devoted and sweetly loving; the merman prince in the Breton story, *Margrette*, has a heart of gold; and the merman in the Arabian story, *The Four Abdallahs*, is a thoroughly good fellow.

One advantage which these sea people have over mere mortals is their capacity for breathing equally comfortably under water or on land. To many of them this capacity for under-and-over-water breathing is innate; others need a special talisman to accomplish it. *The Untidy Mermaid*, for instance, can't go back under the sea once she has lost her magic belt. And the mermaids of Scotland and Ireland possess a little cocked hat, which they take off when they come on land, and put on again when they go back into the sea. So that what with their hats, belts, combs and looking glasses, it seems that mermaids have plenty of luggage to carry about with them.

A Book of Mermaids

Sven & Lilli

There was a little lad called Sven and he lived by the sea. So one day he took his father's boat and went fishing. But the wind blew up and the waves rose high, and the boat turned upside down; and there was Sven struggling in the water. He caught hold of the boat, but he couldn't right it, so he climbed on to the upturned keel, and clung there with the waves washing over him; and the boat drifted and drifted till he lost sight of land.

'Oh, oh!' he cried. 'What shall I do? There's no road home! What shall I do?'

And up swam a whale and said, 'Little boy, why are you crying?'

'Oh, oh, I'm lost! There's no road home!'

'I know the road,' said the whale. 'Come, sit on my back.'

'I won't!' cried Sven. 'I'm afraid!'

But a wave washed him off the boat's keel, and then he was glad enough to sit on the whale's back.

The whale swam off, swiftly, swiftly. He didn't go to Sven's home; he went to his own home under the sea. It was a big, domed, stone house. The walls were of red granite, and the steps of yellow granite.

In the house Sven saw the whale's little daughter, whose name was Lilli. She was a beautiful little mermaid: her eyes were like stars, her hair shone like the sun, her body was like mother of pearl, and she had a golden tail.

Said the whale, 'Lilli, do you like this boy?'

'Yes, I like him; let him stay.'

Said the whale, 'Sven, would you like to stay and wait upon Lilli?'

'Yes, I will stay,'

So Sven became Lilli's servant.

Lilli said, 'Sven, what work can you do?'

'I can hoe turnips.'

'Bah! We haven't any turnips. What else can you do?'

'I can steer a boat.'

'Bah! We don't want boats. What other work do you know?'

'I can catch fish.'

'Oh, oh, you mustn't do that! We love fish. My father is king over all the fishes. Well, never mind. Comb my hair.'

So Sven combed Lilli's hair, and that was all the work he did. He and Lilli spent their time playing. They laughed and joked together; and when they grew old enough, they married.

One day Sven said, 'How is it, Lilli, that you haven't a looking glass, although your face is so nice?'

Lilli said, 'I want a looking glass. Get me one.'

Sven said, 'In my parents' house there is a looking glass, but I don't know the way there.'

Lilli said, 'I know the way. Get on my back. I'll take you there.'

So Sven got on Lilli's back, and she swam with him away and away, till they came to a stony shore. Beyond the shore Sven saw the village and the house where he was born.

Lilli said, 'You must go on alone now. I can't walk in your country. I will sit on this rock under the shallow water and wait for you. But come back quickly!'

'Yes, I will come back quickly,' Sven said. And he slid off Lilli's back and waded through the shallows and went up the beach to his parents' house.

He opened the door and went in. His mother was standing at a table under the window, making pastry.

'Who are you? And what do you want?'

'I am Sven. I have come for a looking glass for my wife.'

'You are not Sven! Sven was drowned ten years back. Go away!'

'Mother, indeed I am Sven. Look at my face.'

His mother looked long at his face, and shook her head.

'My Sven had a brown funny face, crinkled up with laughter. Your face is smooth and fair, and shines like the moon. No, you are not Sven! Go away!'

'Mother, give me your looking glass, and I will go.'

'I will give you nothing. Be off!'

And she threw the rolling pin at him.

Then Sven's father came in. 'Who are you, and what are you doing here?'

'I am Sven. I have come for a looking glass.'

And he told them how he was married to Lilli, the mermaid.

A likely story! No! They wouldn't believe him.

'Be off with you!' His father took up the poker and drove him out of the house.

So Sven went to his grandmother's house, and she was sitting by the fire, knitting a stocking.

'Who are you? What do you want?'

'Granny, I am Sven. Will you give me your looking glass?'

'Sven was drowned ten years ago. You are not Sven!'

'No, I wasn't drowned. I married a mermaid. She has a nice face, and needs a looking glass.'

'You are lying to me! You shan't have my looking glass. I need it myself. I am not yet so old and ugly that I can do without a glass. Be off with you!'

And she threw the stocking at him.

So Sven went to his great-grandmother's house; and she was rocking herself in a chair, twiddling her thumbs and singing to herself.

'Good morning, Great-Grandmother!'

'Who are you, and what have you come for?'

'I am Sven. I tumbled into the sea and married a mermaid. She has a pretty face, Great-Granny; she needs a looking glass.'

'Yes, you are Sven. Give me a kiss! You can have my looking glass. What do I want with it?'

The looking glass was hanging on the wall. Sven was going to take it down, when his girl cousin came in.

'Who is this man? What is he doing here?'

'He is Sven. He has come for my looking glass.'

'No, he is not Sven—Sven was drowned! He can't have that looking glass. You promised it to me!'

'I never did!'

'Well, I want it. I'm going to be married next week. A newly wedded wife needs a looking glass, so that she may keep herself tidy and please her husband.'

But Sven took the looking glass and ran off with it.

His girl cousin ran after him, screaming, 'Thief! Thief! Thief!' And her sweetheart heard, and her brothers heard. They took sticks and ran after Sven, and beat him, and took the looking glass from him, and left him lying as one dead at the top of the beach.

Lilli sat on the rock under the shallow water. She waited, waited. Sven did not come. She began to sing and call, 'Come back, Sven! Come back, Sven!'

But Sven did not come.

So Lilli lifted her head up above the shallow water. She saw Sven lying as one dead at the top of the beach. And she gave a cry: 'Father, send me a wave! Send me a great wave, Father!'

So the whale sent a great wave, and the wave lifted Lilli, and floated her up the beach to where Sven lay.

Lilli took Sven in her arms, and the wave ran back, and carried them again into the shallow water. Sven opened his eyes and said, 'I am greatly hurt, my Lilli, and they have taken the looking glass from me.'

Then Lilli sparkled with anger, and she cried out, 'Send me huge waves, Father! Huge waves to drown this village!'

And the whale sent huge waves. They roared up the beach and dashed upon the houses, tumbling them right and left. The people all fled to the hill behind the village; the girl cousin fled; the girl's sweetheart put down the looking glass and fled; the girl's brothers dropped their sticks and fled; Sven's mother left her pastry and fled; Sven's father caught up the grandmother and fled. But no-one thought of the great-grandmother. The walls of her house fell down; the roof fell in; the waves lifted her rocking chair, and there she was, rocking on the top of the waves in her chair, twiddling her thumbs and singing to herself.

Then the whale called the waves, and the waves fell back; and as they went they set the great-grandmother softly down on the beach in her chair. And the looking glass, which the girl's sweetheart had dropped, lay at her feet. So she called out, 'Sven! Sven! Here is your looking glass! Come and take it!'

But Sven couldn't come: he was too badly hurt.

So Lilli sang out, 'Father, send us a wave! Send us a little wave, Father, to carry us up the beach to the great-grandmother's feet!'

And the whale sent a gentle little wave to carry Lilli and Sven up to the feet of the great-grandmother. And the great-grandmother rocked and twiddled her thumbs, and said, 'Give me a kiss, my pretty one, you who are Sven's wife. Take the looking glass. And here in my pocket is some ointment to rub Sven's hurt away.'

Lilli kissed the great-grandmother, and took the looking glass and the ointment. And the wave carried Lilli and Sven back into the sea; and Lilli swam home with Sven clasped in her arms.

When the sea was all quiet, the people came down from the hill, and began to build up their houses. The great-grandmother watched them as she rocked in her chair and twiddled her thumbs.

'You had been wiser if you had been kinder,' she said.

And down under the sea in the domed house, Lilli rubbed Sven's hurts with the great-grandmother's ointment, and he grew well and strong again. He combed Lilli's hair and said, 'Look in the glass, my Lilli, and see what a nice face you have.'

Lilli looked in the glass and said, 'Yes, I have a nice face, my Sven.'

Sven combed Lilli's hair every day, and every day she looked in the glass and smiled. They lived happily. And there, in their domed house under the sea, so people say, they are living still.

2

The Lost Prince

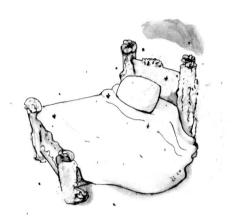

There was a prince and he went out to hunt with his courtiers. But a mist blew up from the sea and hid each man from his fellow, and when the mist cleared, the prince had vanished. The courtiers ran about searching. They searched and called, searched and called—all no use, not a trace of the prince. So they went back to the palace and told the king.

The king grew sick with grief and took to his bed. He said he would give half his kingdom to any one who could find the prince; he sent out heralds calling the news into every part of his kingdom. Then many a man set off to look for the prince. But no man found him.

Now in a far away corner of the kingdom there lived a pretty girl. The girl lived with her father and mother in a wretched little hovel, and they were very, very poor. The girl thought, 'What a fine thing it would be for us, if *I* could find the prince! Oh, I wouldn't be greedy; I wouldn't ask half the kingdom, nor a quarter of it, nor an eighth, nor a sixteenth. I would only ask for a little farm where my poor old father and mother could live in peace and comfort.'

So she told her parents she was off to look for the prince.

'But bless me first,' said she, 'for I can't go without your blessing.'

Her parents didn't want her to go, but go she would—no help for it. So they gave her their blessing, and what food they could spare, and off she went.

The places that girl went to, you wouldn't believe. Up over frozen mountains she went, down into thorny valleys, across wild wildernesses, and through forests where no man had ever trod. She walked the shoes off her feet, and went on barefoot: she walked her clothes into rags, pinned the rags together with thorns from the hedge, and walked on. Did she find the prince? No, she did not. And at last, when there was no place left in the kingdom for her to search, she went and sat on the sea shore.

'The prince is surely dead and underground,' she thought. 'I may as well go home.'

'Ha! ha! ha!' Someone was laughing. She looked up. It was a whale laughing at her. He had his head up out of the sea, and his mouth was all one grin.

'I don't think you ought to laugh at me,' said the girl. 'I'm tired out and disappointed, and I can't find what I'm looking for. Is that funny?'

The whale said, 'Yes, it is funny. Because you've been looking in the wrong places.'

'I've looked everywhere!'

'No, you haven't. I know where the right place is.'

'Oh where? Where?'

'Are you a good swimmer?'

'No.'

'Then you must get on my back, and I'll carry you.'

The girl got on the whale's back, and he swam out to sea. He was all day and all night going. And at last he came to a little island with a great cave in it.

'This is the right place,' said the whale. 'Get down now, and go into the cave.'

The girl got down from the whale's back. The whale swam away. And the girl went into the cave.

The cave was long and dark, but at the far end of it something was glittering. The girl groped her way towards the glitter, and there she found two beds. One bed was covered with cloth of silver, and the other with cloth of gold. And whom did she see lying on the gold bed, fast asleep, but the prince she was looking for.

On the head of the bed there were carved some magic words. The girl couldn't read them, but she didn't waste time over them, she was too busy trying to wake the prince. She called him, she shook him, she pinched him; no good—he wouldn't wake. Then she tried kissing him, for she remembered that there was charm in a maiden's kiss: not a bit of good, there was no charm in *her* kiss, it seemed, to waken anybody.

She was still trying, when she heard a spatter of foam at the opening of the cave. Someone coming! The girl ran to hide in the darkest corner, behind a jutting rock. And in came a mermaid.

The mermaid was sparkling all over, for she was covered with gold and silver scales; and her long golden hair was dripping with water that made pools on the cave floor. Oh well, she lit up the cave with her beauty; but she didn't light up the corner behind the rock where the girl hid.

The mermaid went up to the sleeping prince and looked down on him. From a shelf she took rare sea fruits and bright drinks in silver goblets. She set these things on a table at the foot of the prince's bed. Then she put her fingers to her mouth and whistled.

What did the girl see then? She saw two white swans swimming into the cave through the pools where the mermaid's hair had dripped. They swam to the foot of the bed, and the mermaid said:

> '*Sing, sing, my swans,*
> *That the king's son may wake.*'

And the swans sang, and the prince rubbed his eyes and sat up, wide awake.

'Eat,' said the mermaid.

'No,' said the prince.

'How long will you be stubborn?' said the mermaid. 'In the end you shall love me and marry me.'

'I will never love you!' said the prince.

So the mermaid spoke to the swans again:

> '*Sing, sing, my swans,*
> *That the king's son may sleep.*'

And the swans sang, and the prince yawned, and lay down again on the golden bed, and fell asleep.

The mermaid ate of the rare sea fruits and drank of the bright drinks, and then she lay down on the silver bed and slept. The swans put their heads under their wings and slept also. All was quiet. The girl crept out from the dark corner where she was hiding, and ate a little of the sea fruits, and drank a little of the bright drink. And then she hid herself again; but she did not sleep.

In the morning the mermaid woke, and the swans woke; but the prince slept on. The mermaid said to the swans:

> 'Sing, sing, my swans,
> That the king's son may wake.'

And the swans sang, and the prince woke up.

'Eat,' said the mermaid.

'No,' said the prince.

'Today you shall love me and marry me,' said the mermaid.

But the prince answered, 'The world shall come to an end before I love you.'

So then the mermaid bade the swans put him to sleep again. And after that, she went out of the cave, and the swans followed her.

The girl came out of her dark corner, and looked down at the sleeping prince. How beautiful he was, as he lay there sleeping! She scarcely dared to wake him. But she put her fingers to her lips and whistled, and the swans came in. Said the girl:

'Sing, sing, my swans,
That the kings son may wake.'

And the swans sang.

The prince sat up, rubbed his eyes, and said, 'Who are you?'

'A poor girl who has come seeking you.'

And she told him about the king's grieving, and about the proclamation, and about her journeying and seeking, and about the whale who had brought her to the cave.

'But you,' she said, 'how did you come here?'

So he told her of the hunting and of the mist that blew in from the sea, hiding each man from his fellows. And in that mist he had heard his courtiers calling. So he ran in the direction of their voices, and the earth slipped away from under him, and he fell into nothingness. With the swiftness of that fall he swooned, and when he came to himself he was in the mermaid's arms.

'She kissed me and flattered me and bade me love her. But still I said "no." So she brought me to this cave and laid me on this golden bed and put me to sleep. Every morning and every evening she wakes me and bids me eat and love her; and always I say "no", and she puts me to sleep again. And so it seems that I must wake and sleep, wake and sleep, till doomsday.'

'Not so,' said the girl. 'I'll help you to escape. But here is food, so let us eat together.'

So they ate of the rare sea fruits. The prince looked at the girl and smiled. 'You are very lovely, my little one,' he said.

The girl looked at the prince and smiled. She thought him more lovely than the sun and the moon and the stars and all beautiful things rolled into one. But she said nothing. She remembered that she was a poor girl, and that he was a prince.

'And how shall we escape from here?' said the prince.

The girl said, 'You must pretend to agree with the mermaid. Eat of the food and drink of the drink she offers. And when she speaks of love and marriage, do not say her nay. Only bid her wait until tomorrow evening. And above all, ask her what she does by day, and what is the meaning of the magical words written on the bed.'

'I will do as you bid me,' said the prince; 'for it seems to me that you are very wise, my little one.'

'And now,' said the girl, 'I must put you to sleep.'

She whistled to the swans, and they came and she said,

> 'Sing, sing, my swans,
> That the king's son may sleep.'

The swans sang; the prince fell asleep; the swans went away, and the girl hid in the dark corner behind the rock.

In the evening the mermaid came dripping into the cave, called the swans, and woke the prince. Then she looked at the table and said, 'Some one has been eating! Some one has been drinking!'

The prince laughed. 'I couldn't eat and drink in my sleep,' said he. 'But I feel strangely happy, and I am willing to eat now.'

'Then it was you swans who have been eating and drinking!' cried the mermaid. 'How dare you?' And she threatened to kill them.

But the swans stretched out their necks and ruffled up their wings and hissed at her. So the mermaid said, 'Well, I will forgive you this once.' She knew she couldn't do without them. And she was really in a good temper because the prince had said he was happy and had agreed to eat. So she took down more food from the shelf and the prince ate and drank.

'And now you will love me and marry me?' said the mermaid.

'Wait until tomorrow,' said the prince, 'for now I am tired. Put me to sleep, and let me sleep undisturbed until tomorrow evening. If you wake me then, I will marry you. But what do you do all day whilst I am sleeping?'

'I go near to the haunts of men,' said the mermaid. 'I rise up from the sea, sit on a rock and comb my hair and sing. I watch the comings and goings of you human creatures. And when I see a beautiful youth I draw him down to me. But I have found none more beautiful than you; and if tomorrow night you will become my husband, I shall seek no more. Now you shall sleep.'

'But tell me first the meaning of the words written on the head of my bed,' said the prince.

'Oh nothing much,' said she. 'They say,

> *Run, run, my little bed,*
> *Run whither I will.'*

'And will the bed run if you tell it to?'

'It will,' said the mermaid. 'But why should it, since this cave is home? Now sleep.'

So the swans sang, and the prince slept; the mermaid lay down on the silver bed and slept; the swans put their heads under their wings and slept. And the girl curled herself up in her dark corner, and slept also.

In the morning the mermaid didn't wake the prince. She had promised him that he should sleep till evening. She went out of the cave and the swans followed her. But the girl put her fingers to her mouth and whistled them back. Said the girl:

> 'Sing, sing, my swans,
> Sing that the king's son may wake.'

And the swans sang, and the prince woke.

Then the girl got on to the golden bed beside the prince, and said,

> 'Run, run, my little bed,
> Run whither I will.'

And at once the bed moved out of the cave, and over the rocks to the sea. And across the sea it carried them, straight and swiftly, like any good little ship.

'We are saved!' cried the prince.

'I don't know,' said the girl. 'Look back.'

The prince looked back. All round the island the sea was boiling and foaming. For the mermaid had returned to the cave to adorn herself for her wedding; and when she saw that the prince was gone and the bed was gone, her rage was terrible. Round the island she rushed searching, beating up the sea in her wrath, and screaming,

> 'Bed, bed, my little bed,
> Tell where you have gone!'

And the bed, because it could do no other, answered from across the water,

> 'I am here, I am running away,
> I am running away swiftly.'

Then the mermaid wrapped herself in a huge wave; and the huge wave rose up green and roaring and rushed over the sea to swamp the bed. But the girl saw the wave coming and she cried out, 'Oh friend whale, you helped me once, help me now again!'

And the whale rose in wrath and rushed to meet the mermaid, and seized her by the hair, and they fought together till the whole ocean was lashed to fury. Winds howled, waves leaped; the bed spun round and round, water washed over it, the prince and the girl clung to the head of the bed, and the prince cried out, 'We sink! We sink! Oh that this bed could fly!'

'Who knows? Perhaps it can,' thought the girl. And she called,

> 'Fly, fly, my little bed,
> Fly whither I will.'

At once the bed rose in the air, and sped on swiftly above the raging of the sea.

When the mermaid saw the bed flying, she knew she was beaten. She couldn't fly; it was no use trying. She ceased to fight the whale. The whale gave her one last shake, and let her go. She swam back to her lonely cave, to sit and weep there. The waves stilled themselves, the winds stopped howling; the sea lay like a crystal mirror. And over that crystal mirror the little bed went flying, flying, till it brought the prince and the girl safe to shore. So, when they had landed, the girl said,

> *'Fly, fly, my little bed,*
> *Fly whither you will.'*

And the bed flew back to the mermaid.

'Goodbye, my prince,' said the girl then. 'Greet your father the king from me, and tell him I don't ask for half the kingdom; I ask only a small farm where my old parents may live in peace and comfort.'

'Is that all you ask,' cried the prince, 'you who have saved my life? Come with me to my father's court!'

'You are a prince,' said she, 'and I am a poor girl; I cannot come with you.'

Said he, 'I am poorer than the poorest if you leave me. I am richer than the richest if you will be my wife. I love you. Can you not love me?'

'I can,' said the girl, 'and I do.'

'Then give me your hand and we will go together to the king.'

Hand in hand they set off and came to the king's court. The king was still lying sick on his bed; but when he saw the prince he sprang up whole and well. And when the prince told how the girl had saved him, the king cried, 'Half my kingdom! Nay, all of it!'

But the girl didn't want all the kingdom, nor did she want the half of it. She wanted only the prince and comfort for her parents. The prince she got, for they were married next day. Her old parents were fetched to the wedding; and after the wedding the king gave them a pretty little house near the palace, and there they lived in comfort.

As for the girl and the prince, they were so happy that no one has ever been happier. And happy they remained ever after.

3

The Three Mermaids

Once upon a time there was a rich widower who had an only daughter, called Cecilia. Cecilia was pretty and good; and if the widower had been content to stay as he was, all would have been well. But what must he go and do but marry a widow, who also had an only daughter. Grannizia was the daughter's name, and she was not pretty or good; neither was the widow: they were both ugly and envious.

As soon as he was married, the man knew what a mistake he had made. The new wife made his life a burden: she bullied, she scolded, she must have her own way in everything, right or wrong. She was a terror, and every day she got worse. At last the man could stand it no longer. One early morning he packed a few things in a bag, slung the bag over his shoulder, and stole out of the house.

Cecilia saw him going and ran after him.

'Father, father, where are you going?'

'My poor child, I am going away. I am leaving everything to your stepmother. I will find some work or other, and make a new home. And when I have a new home, I will send for you. Don't cry, my little bird; soon we shall be together again.'

Cecilia waited and waited. But her father didn't send for her. The work he found would barely keep himself: he had no money to make a new home. And the stepmother was furious. She was glad enough to be rid of her husband, but she had to blame someone for his leaving her; and she blamed Cecilia. First she gave Cecilia a good beating; then she snatched off her pretty clothes and dressed her in rags; then she put her to do all the dirty work. But she dressed her own daughter, Grannizia, in fine clothes, and made Cecilia wait on her. And Grannizia gave herself airs, and looked down on Cecilia.

The house where they lived was on a cliff above the sea; and one day the stepmother sent Cecilia out with a bucket of garbage to empty over the cliff. The bucket was very heavy, and as Cecilia stooped over the cliff edge to shake out the garbage, the bucket slipped from her hands, and went rattle, rattle, rattle down the cliff, and bump! on to the beach below.

Oh dear, oh dear! Cecilia knew that if she went back without the bucket, her stepmother would give her a beating. What was she to do? The cliff was very high and steep. She knelt down and peered over it: there was the bucket lying on the sand, and lying with his tail curled round the bucket was a sea-monster. The sea-monster had huge eyes that glittered like green gems, and he was staring up at Cecilia.

Cecilia felt frightened, but she called down politely, 'Good morning to you, sir!'

'Good morning to you, pretty one, shouted the sea monster. 'What do you wish?'

'I wish you many blessings, sir,' said Cecilia. 'I wish you a rich wife and all that your heart can desire. And if you could climb up to me with my bucket, I should be greatly obliged.'

'My good girl,' said the sea monster, 'if you want your bucket, you must come and fetch it.' And he got up, twitched his tail, and waddled off into the sea on his flat webbed feet.

So Cecilia, holding tight to roots and stones, began to scramble down the cliff face. The stones broke loose, the roots came away in her hands, she all but fell many a time; but she got down at last. She was about to pick up her bucket (though how she would get up that cliff again, she didn't know) when she heard the sound of very sweet singing. And there, under the cliff, she saw a cave, and in it were three mermaids, singing and combing their hair.

'Come hither, come hither, you pretty little girl!' sang the mermaids. So Cecilia went into the cave, and the mermaids bade her sit down by them.

'Now we have a pretty little girl to comb for us,' said the first mermaid. And she laid her head in Cecilia's lap and said, 'Comb! Comb!' Cecilia combed the mermaid's hair, and the mermaid said, 'You look at my hair, and what do you see?'

'I see sunbeams in it,' said Cecilia.

'Is it beautiful and gold and shining?' said the mermaid.

'It is beautiful and gold and shining as the sun itself,' said Cecilia.

Then the second mermaid laid her head in Cecilia's lap and said, 'Comb! Comb!'

Cecilia combed the second mermaid's hair, and the second mermaid said, 'You look at my hair and what do you see?'

"I see moonbeams in it,' said Cecilia.

'Is it beautiful, silver, and shining?' said the second mermaid.

"It is beautiful, silver, and shining as the full moon itself,' said Cecilia.

The third mermaid laid her head in Cecilia's lap, and said, 'Comb! Comb!'

So Cecilia combed, and the third mermaid said, 'You look at my hair and what do you see?'

"I see starlight in it," said Cecilia.

'Is it beautiful and bright and shining?' said the third mermaid.

'It is beautiful and bright, and it shines like the stars in heaven,' said Cecilia.

The three mermaids were pleased. They looked at their hair in their mirrors and said, 'Yes, little girl, you have done very well! And you have the manners of a princess. Come, we will show you our house.'

They took her down under the cave, and swam with her through emerald green water into a palace of pearl, very grand and beautiful. They brought her lovely clothes and jewels and said, 'Choose which you will have.'

But Cecilia said, 'I am not used to grand clothes. But I see I have torn and dirtied my apron coming down the cliff. So if you have an apron to spare that is neat and plain, I should be grateful.'

'Listen to her!" laughed the mermaids. 'An apron, neat and plain!

Has no one ever told you, child, how beautiful you are? You are beautiful as any queen, and queenly shall be your raiment.'

And they brought a gold dress and put it on her. Then they combed her hair with their golden combs till it glittered like the morning dew. And they set on her head the prettiest little hat like a basket of flowers, tied it with flowery ribbons under her chin, knotted up some of her hair on top, and left the rest to hang down in curls each side. Then they brought her to stand in front of a looking glass.

'Can this really be myself?' said Cecilia. 'Or is it a princess?'

'Both! Both!' cried the mermaids.

And they laughed and kissed her.

'Now you must take your bucket and go home,' they told her. 'Which way will you go, by the front door or the back?'

There was a big golden door at the front of the palace; and there was a little wooden stable door at the back of the palace.

'I will go out the back way,' said Cecilia.

But the mermaids laughed again, and pushed her out through the golden door, and as she was going through it, they called, 'Look up! Look up! See what is above you!'

Cecilia looked up; and a golden star fell from the lintel of the door on to her forehead.

As soon as she had gone through the door she found herself on the top of the cliff with the bucket in her hand. The bucket felt heavy. She looked down. It was full to the brim with pearls.

'Oh, my stepmother will be pleased with me at last!' she thought. And she ran into the house.

But when her stepmother saw her in her golden dress, with the flowery hat on her head and her hair in elegant curls, and the golden star shining on her forehead—well, then the stepmother wasn't pleased at all. She screamed with rage.

'What have you been up to—stealing?' she screamed. 'How dare you come into the house dressed like that? And what's that ridiculous thing on your forehead? Take it off! Take everything off!'

She snatched the hat from Cecilia's head, and stripped her of the golden dress. She tried to pull the star from Cecilia's forehead, too; but all she did was to burn her fingers. And that made her angrier than ever. But when she saw the bucket full of pearls, she calmed down and said, 'Well, after all, I see you haven't been wasting your time.' And she emptied the pearls into a chest and locked them up, and bade Cecilia tell where she had got them.

So Cecilia told her, and the stepmother said, 'Tomorrow Grannizia shall go. If the mermaids gave riches to a miserable little shrimp like you, they will give my Grannizia twice as much.'

'What, me go down that dreadful cliff?' said Grannizia. 'I won't do it!'

'You will do as I tell you,' said the stepmother.

So, the next morning, she put two buckets into Grannizia's hands, took her by the arm and hustled her to the edge of the cliff. Then she snatched the buckets and threw them over the cliff, rattle, rattle, rattle, bump, bump! on to the shore below.

'Down with you after them!' she said to Grannizia.

Grannizia dug her heels into the turf at the top of the cliff, and cried, 'I won't—I won't!' But the stepmother gave her a push, and over she went, sliding and scrambling, and clinging to whatever there was to cling to, and came to the bottom bruised and angry.

The mermaids were singing in their cave. They called to Grannizia to come in: and in she marched and sat down by them.

'Here, give me a golden comb, and look sharp about it!' she said. 'It seems I have to comb your hair. I don't see why I should, but I suppose I must!'

They gave her the comb. The first mermaid laid her head in Grannizia's lap, and said, 'Comb! Comb!'

Grannizia dragged the comb through the mermaid's hair, and the mermaid said, 'You comb, you comb, you are rough in your combing. You look on my hair, and what do you see?'

'I see bits of green seaweed, all tangled up,' said Grannizia.

Then the second mermaid laid her head in Grannizia's lap and said, 'Comb! Comb!'

Grannizia jerked the comb through the mermaid's hair, and the mermaid said, 'You comb, you comb, you are not kind in your combing! You look on my hair, and what do you see?'

'I see ropes of brown seaweed all stuck together,' said Grannizia. 'Don't blame me if your comb breaks!'

The third mermaid laid her head in Grannizia's lap, and Grannizia tugged the comb through her shining hair.

'You comb, you comb,' said the third mermaid. 'You are rough and cruel in your combing. You look at my hair and what do you see?'

'I see rags of cloth washed up by the tide and full of sand,' said Grannizia. 'There, that's done! Now let's have a look at your gems and your fine dresses. For that's why I've come—to be dressed up smartly and get two buckets full of pearls.'

The mermaids took Grannizia down through the emerald green water to their palace of pearl. They brought out their lovely dresses and jewels, and said, 'Choose!'

But Grannizia flung the jewels from her and stamped on the dresses.

'Is this the best you can do?' she said. 'You don't get rid of me so easily! I am not going till I have a much finer dress, and far more splendid jewels than you gave to that little kitchen wench Cecilia.'

The mermaids showed her every dress they had, and still Grannizia demanded better and finer ones.

'We have no more,' said the mermaids at last.

'Then I suppose I must take the best of a bad lot,' said Grannizia. And she chose a dress all weighted down with huge rubies. The dress was so stiff that when she put it on she could hardly move, and she didn't look at all nice in it.

Then she searched around for a head-dress. There was a crown of pearls, a tiara of diamonds, a chaplet of emeralds. She crammed them on her head one on top of the other, and said, 'I'll take the lot.'

The mermaids led her to stand in front of the looking glass. They were laughing like anything.

'What are you laughing at?' said Grannizia.

'Oh nothing! nothing!' they said, and went on laughing.

'I should like to box the ears of all three of you, you rude things!' said Grannizia. 'I'm going now. Where are my buckets?'

'Here.'

'Have you filled them with pearls?' said Grannizia.

'They are quite full and heavy,' said the mermaids.

The buckets were so full of pearls that Grannizia could hardly lift them. What with the heavy buckets, and the heavy dress, and the heavy crowns on her head, she had a job to walk.

'Open the door for me,' she said, staggering along.

'The big golden door, or the little wooden one?' they asked.

'The golden one, of course!' said Grannizia. 'Am I an ass that I should go out through your stables?'

The mermaids opened the golden door, and as Grannizia was going through it, they called out, 'Look up! Look up! See what is above you!'

'Oh, I know all about what's above me,' said Grannizia. 'I was going to look up without you telling me.'

Did she know what was above her? Not she! When she looked up, a donkey's tail fell from the lintel of the door on to her forehead.

There she was now, standing on the top of the cliff outside her home. She tried to pull the donkey's tail off her forehead, but it stuck fast, as if it grew there. She put up her hand to the crowns on her head: they were ropes of brown seaweed. She looked down at her jewelled dress: it was rags of cloth washed up by the tide and full of sand. She peered into her heavy buckets: they were piled up with beach pebbles. She flung the buckets down outside the door, and ran in howling.

Grannizia howled, the stepmother screamed, poor little Cecilia put her hands over her ears and crept away into a corner. But the stepmother dragged her out, and shook her.

'This is all your doing!' screamed the stepmother. 'Take the pig swill and off to the sties with you! What the pigs leave you can eat, and where the pigs lie, you can lie. You'll get nothing more in this house, either food or bed!'

Cecilia took the pails of pig swill and went out. The stepmother stripped off Grannizia's rags, and dressed her in the clothes the mermaids had given to Cecilia. But she couldn't wrench the donkey's tail from Grannizia's forehead, however much she tugged and twisted. She took a knife to cut it off, but Grannizia howled, 'No, no, leave it alone! It hurts! It hurts!'

So then the stepmother fetched Cecilia's flowery hat, tipped it well forward over Grannizia's brow, twisted the tail up under the hat, and looped her hair about it. 'Now it scarcely shows,' she said. 'But one of these days I shall kill that Cecilia!'

Cecilia spent the night in the pig sties. She felt cold in her rags, but the pigs were friendly; they crowded round her and kept her warm. In the morning, when she led the pigs out into the fields, she heard the sound of galloping hoofs, and a horseman came riding along the road on the other side of the hedge. Cecilia looked up at the horseman; he was indeed worth looking at: he was a prince, no other. The prince looked down at Cecilia. The golden star shone on her brow, and though she was in rags, her beauty was bright as the morning.

'Where is your home, little beauty?' he asked.

'In the pig sty, sir,' said she.

'And who owns the pigs?'

'My stepmother, sir,' said she.

'And where does your stepmother live?'

'In yonder house, sir,' said she.

'If I get your stepmother's consent, will you be my wife?'

'Willingly, sir,' said she.

The prince turned his horse and rode to the house.

'Is any one within?'

The stepmodier came out. She was all smiles and curtseys.

'I am a prince. Will you give me your stepdaughter for wife—the lovely girl with the star on her forehead?'

The stepmother bobbed and grinned, 'If you will send for her to-night, your highness, I will get her ready.'

'I will come for her tonight,' said the prince, and rode away.

The stepmother called Grannizia. 'We must do what we can with you,' she said. 'The prince comes tonight to marry you.'

She hurried into town and bought a pot of gold paint. She painted a gold star on the piece of the donkey's tail that showed under the flowery hat. 'By night the prince won't know any difference,' she said. 'And once you are married he'll have to put up with you.'

In the evening the prince came back. It was a dark night, the moon was not yet risen, and only a star or two showed amongst the clouds. When Grannizia heard the prince calling, she opened the door of the house and stepped out into the darkness. The prince couldn't see her face. But the gold paint gleamed under the brim of the hat, and the gold dress that the mermaids had given to Cecilia glittered.

'Are you ready, my bride?' said the prince.

'I am dressed and ready,' said Grannizia.

'Your voice sounds strangely different,' said the prince.

'I am a little husky—it is the cold night air,' said she.

The prince swung her up on his horse and galloped away with her. At dawn he galloped her back.

One glance when they got to the palace had shown him how he had been deceived. Now he was looking everywhere for Cecilia; but he couldn't find her. The stepmother had gone to the forest to gather sticks. And where was Cecilia? Shut up in a barrel with the lid nailed firmly down on top of her. The stepmother was gathering sticks to make a bonfire and burn that barrel.

The prince had searched in the fields, he had searched in the pig sties. Now he was running through the house, searching in every room. 'My bride! My bride!' he called. 'Where are you?'

The barrel stood in the kitchen by the ashes of the hearth. Lying in the ashes was a tabby cat. 'Miaow! Miaow!' said the tabby cat.

'My bride! My bride, where are you?' cried the prince. 'Miaow! Miaow! Your bride is in the barrel,' said the tabby cat.

The prince put his ear against the barrel. He heard a soft, low moaning. He seized a hatchet that hung by the fire, and wrenched up the lid of the barrel. Yes, there inside was his lovely little bride. The prince took her up in his arms, put her on his horse, and galloped away with her.

The stepmother came back with the firewood. What did she see? She saw the barrel lying on its side, and Grannizia sitting in a corner with her hat in her hand and the donkey's tail hanging down over her nose. 'Miaow! Miaow!' said the tabby cat. 'Our little Cecilia is stolen away.'

The stepmother threw the firewood at the cat. The cat spat at the stepmother. Grannizia howled. The tabby cat marched out of the house with his tail bushed up.

'Miaow! Miaow! I am going to Cecilia's wedding,' he said.

It was a very grand wedding. The three mermaids were invited. They came riding on the sea monster. The sea monster gave a wink with one of his huge green eyes and said to Cecilia, 'You did right, my good girl, to climb down the cliff after your bucket.'

The mermaids gave Cecilia three wishes.

Cecilia's first wish was that they would take the donkey's tail off Grannizia's forehead.

The second wish was that her father might be found and brought to live at the palace.

The third wish was that everyone might be as happy as she was.

The first two wishes the mermaids granted at once. And if they couldn't quite grant Cecilia's third wish, they did their best. At any rate they saw to it that most people were happy. And if there were any people who weren't happy—well, that was not the mermaids' fault.

4

Rake Up!

Once upon a time there was a mermaid who kept a herd of sea-grey cows, and a huge bull, called Mark.

One day the cows said to the mermaid, 'We eat and eat and eat, and always the same seaweedy trash. If you don't give us a change of food, our milk will dry up.'

And the huge bull, Mark, said, 'The cows speak truly. What they need is grass.'

Now the mermaid knew that beyond the shore there was a wide stretch of good green grass. So, riding very queenly on the foremost cow, she led her herd out of the water, up over the sandy beach, and on to the grass. Said she, 'Now, my darling grey cows, and you, my huge bull Mark, eat your fill.'

The cows and Mark grazed on that stretch of grass all day; and the mermaid sat on a stone near by, and sang to them, and combed her hair.

Beyond the green grass was a little town. And when the people in the town saw the grey cows and the huge bull eating up the grass, and the mermaid sitting on a stone, combing her hair and singing, they were as angry as could be. And that was very wrong and selfish of them, because they hadn't any cattle themselves, and the grass was just waste; so the mermaid wasn't doing any harm by letting her cattle graze there. But it was just the way they were, these people: if *they* couldn't make use of the grass, then nobody else should!

And in the evening they took sticks and stones, and ran round between the mermaid and the sea, so that she couldn't take her cattle back into the water; and they beat that poor mermaid, and set on the cows with their sticks and stones. The huge bull, Mark, was bellowing like trumpets, and he would have made mincemeat of the whole lot of those people, but the mermaid forbade him.

'No, no, my good Mark, that is not the way to behave!' she said, for she was queenly in her manners. 'Let the people be; it will all come right in the end.'

So Mark stopped his bellowing, because he always did what the mermaid told him: and the people drove the whole lot of them, cows, bull, mermaid and all, up into the town, and shut them in a yard with a great gate to it. Then they locked the gate and went away, and held a meeting to decide what to do next.

'Kill the lot!' said one man, and he was the butcher.

But another man, and he was the tailor, said, 'No, no, we can't do that! What about that monstrous bull? What about his long sharp horns? He'd gore the life out of us before he'd let us touch one of the cows!'

Then a third man, and he was the lawyer, said, 'Don't mermaids possess riches? And haven't her cattle eaten down grass that doesn't belong to her? Make her pay damages!'

And all the people cheered and said, 'Yes, yes, that's what we'll do! Make her pay damages—and heavy ones!'

So in the morning, they went to the mermaid and told her they wouldn't let her go until she had paid them for the grass.

The mermaid said, 'I can't pay. I haven't any money.'

'A likely story! A mermaid and no money! What about that girdle of pearls and rubies and diamonds you're wearing?'

'Oh,' said the mermaid, 'you're welcome to that.'

Now the mermaid's girdle was most magnificent, gleaming with jewels—pearls, rubies, and diamonds, bigger ones than any man of them had ever seen in his life. And they thought, 'If we take those jewels to the city and sell them, we shall all be rich to the end of our days.' But they were so greedy that still they wanted more.

So they went aside and debated, and came to the mermaid again, and said, 'Give us your girdle and you shall go. But only on one condition: that in three days' time you come to the shore where we shall be waiting, and bring us three more such girdles.'

'I will do that,' said the mermaid. She took off her girdle and gave it to them, and they opened the gate of the yard. They were eager to let her go now; for they knew they could trust her to keep her promise about the other three girdles.

45

Riding like a queen on the foremost cow, the mermaid led out her herd; and away they went, very orderly, out of the town, and over the stretch of grass, and down to the sand of the shore. The people stood in a crowd outside the walls of the town to watch them go. The huge bull, Mark, was ambling along behind the cows, quiet as a lamb.

When the herd got down to the water's edge, the mermaid slid from the leading cow's back, and then the cows went into the sea and disappeared, one after the other. Now only the mermaid and the huge bull, Mark, were left on the shore. And the mermaid turned to Mark and said, 'Rake up, my bull!'

The huge bull, Mark, put down his horns and began to rake.

He raked the sand till it flew up in clouds. And still he raked, and still the sand flew up in clouds. It flew up over the green grass and buried it, till not a blade was seen. And still the huge bull raked, and still the sand flew on and on. It swirled up towards the watching people, and buried their feet and filled their eyes and noses. They staggered away before it back to the town, and got into their houses and slammed the doors; and still the huge bull raked, and still the clouds of sand came on and on. The sand lay thick in the streets, it swirled against the windows of the houses, it half buried the church. Soon there would have been nothing left of the town but a great sand heap, if the mermaid hadn't called out, 'Enough, my bull! Stop raking!'

The huge bull, Mark, lifted his head, and gave one bellow, high and clear as a trumpet; and then he followed the mermaid into the sea, and they both disappeared.

The people spent all day shovelling up the sand: hard work it was, and the town looked but a sorry mess when night came and they had to lay down their spades and shovels. Next morning they were at it again, with brooms and buckets, and all as bad tempered as could be: the women howling, the men shouting and cursing.

The lawyer wasn't used to such work; he tired sooner than any one. So he threw down his spade and said, 'What about those jewels? We have *them*, even if the town is a mess. I'll be off to the city now and sell them.'

'You won't go alone!' they all shouted; for not one of them trusted the other. 'The butcher and the tailor must go with you.'

So the three of them set out, the lawyer and the butcher and the tailor, to sell the jewels.

Half way to the city they sat down by a milestone to rest their aching legs: they were worn out with the hard work of clearing up the sand. The lawyer was carrying the mermaid's girdle in a black bag. And as he sat resting, he opened the bag and took out the girdle to gladden his eyes with the sight of the jewels. There lay the girdle now, across his knee, with the great rubies and the huge diamonds and the big pearls gleaming and flashing in the sunlight.

'Thousands of pounds we shall get for these gems!' he said. 'What, only thousands? Nay, millions!'

'Hand that girdle over to me!' said the butcher. 'I shall carry it the rest of the way!'

'No, *I* shall carry it!' said the tailor.

They both snatched at the girdle. The lawyer made to put it back in his bag, but the butcher got hold of one end of it, and the tailor got hold of the other end. They were tugging and scrabbling: the girdle broke, and the rubies and pearls and diamonds rolled into the road.

Rubies and pearls and diamonds? When the three men leaped to gather up those jewels, all they gathered up was a handful of dried seaweed. So they turned and took their weary way back to the town.

On the third day the mermaid came to the edge of the sea. In her hands she had three gleaming girdles. She held them up. The rubies and the diamonds and the pearls flashed in the sunlight. But no man stood on the shore to receive them.

'Here are the three girdles!' called the mermaid.

No one answered. Only, far away on the wall of the town, a man stood up and shook his fist at the sea. It was the lawyer.

'Your girdles!' called the mermaid. 'Come and fetch them!' But no one came. The mermaid tossed the girdles on to the sand. The girdles turned into three little heaps of brown seaweed. And the mermaid laughed, and dived back under the sea.

The Kingdom of Ocean

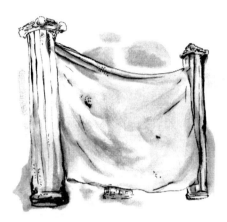

There was a ship and it went sailing across the ocean. But in the midst of the ocean a storm rose up and beat upon the ship, and broke it stem and stern. The ship went down, and all the crew were drowned except one young sailor, who caught at a floating plank and so managed to keep his head above water.

The waves drove the plank on and on, and washed it up at last on a small island. The sailor wrung the water out of his clothes and rested a while. Then he set out to see if he could find any food on the island. He found many trees and shrubs which dazzled him with their beauty; but when he sought to pluck the fruits that hung from them, he found that they were not fruits at all, but sparkling jewels.

'Heaven help me!' he cried. 'What use are these gems to a starving man?' But he gathered a handful and put them in his pocket.

He wandered about the island until sunset, and then he came to a well, and beside the well grew an apple tree. But were those rosy apples really fruits, or were they jewels? He scarcely dared to reach up his hand and pluck one: but hunger raged in him, and he felt that if he couldn't eat, he would die.

Good luck! They were real apples, and he ate till he was full. Then he felt thirsty, stooped over the well, and cupped his hands to drink. And looking down into the well—what did he see? He saw the most beautiful face in the world gazing up at him from the bottom of it. It was a mermaid's face, and there she was, coiled up on her silvery tail and beckoning to him.

He didn't stop to drink, he didn't stop to think, he took a dive, and down he went.

'Welcome to the Kingdom of Ocean!' said the mermaid.

And she took him by the hand and showed him all the wonders of that kingdom; and the richest dream that ever anyone dreamed was not to be compared to the wonders she showed him: golden palaces, sparkling streams, rainbow bridges, green meadows where white sea horses browsed; radiant gardens lit up by flowers that smiled and nodded to him; forests of crystal where brilliantly coloured fishes darted and sang among the branches; caves filled up with diamonds, caves filled up with pearls; caves of rubies, of emeralds, of sapphires; treasure houses of gold and silver—the wealth of that kingdom was beyond all wealth on earth.

'I am queen of this kingdom,' said the mermaid. 'Would you like to be king?'

Would he? Would he not! So the mermaid called her subjects to-gether, and they brought a diamond crown and set it on his head; they wrapped him in a golden cloak, and put silver shoes on his feet, and made him their king.

For a long time the sailor king lived with his mermaid queen in great contentment. Whatever he wanted he had only to wish for; and wherever he wanted to go, he could go in an instant, for the golden cloak spread out like wings and carried him whither he would.

'Is it a happy life you have with me?' said the mermaid.

'It is a very happy life, my queen. But tell me one thing.'

'I will tell you anything,' said she.

'In our palace,' said he, 'there is a hall of pillars. And between two of the pillars there hangs a veil. What is behind that veil?'

'Ah, better you had not asked me!' said she. 'But if you must know, you must.'

So they went together into the hall of pillars; and at the end of the hall there was a veil hung between one pillar and another pil-lar. On the veil there were pictures; the whole world was pictured on that veil, and the pictures moved and changed: forests grew up and faded again; cities rose and fell; new cities rose; ships came and went; rivers flowed and dried up; new rivers flowed; birds sang and were silent; the sun blazed, clouds gathered, snow fell, night came, and dawn again...

'Look on all this,' said the mermaid. 'Is it not enough?'

'No, it is not enough,' said the sailor. 'Let me see what is behind it!'

The mermaid drew the veil aside; and there, high on a pedestal, stood the statue of a little warrior, clad in armour from head to foot.

The sailor put out his hand to touch the statue, but the mermaid cried, 'No, no! To touch is forbidden!' And she drew the veil again in front of the statue, and led the sailor out of the hall of pillars, and said, 'You must promise me that you will never touch that statue.'

'What would happen if I did?' he asked.

'I cannot tell you. I don't know,' she answered.

But he thought she did know; and he wanted to know also. He couldn't get the thought of that little statue out of his mind. He thought about it, he dreamed about it, he went back into the hall of pillars; he drew aside the veil and gazed and gazed at the statue.

'Why shouldn't I touch it?' he said to himself. 'It is only a little image. What harm can a little image do to me, or to anyone?'

And often he lifted his hand to the little statue; and always he drew his hand back again. But he became dissatisfied. The wonderful world he was living in didn't please him any more; the mermaid, with her great love for him, seemed to him silly; his subjects irritated him. 'Am I a king and may I not have my own way?' he thought. 'Am I to bow to the will of a mermaid wife? After all, I promised her nothing. I must and *will* touch that little image, let happen what may!'

So he went into the hall of pillars and drew aside the veil yet once again, and put out his hand to the image and touched one little foot... And the little foot darted forward and gave him a kick, a tremendous kick that sent him flying. Up through the roof of the palace he was hurled, and over the sparkling streams and the rainbow bridges, over the meadows and the gardens and the crystal forests, up, up and away from the Kingdom of Ocean: up through the waters of the well, and across the island and over the seas where he had been wrecked, on and on, and still he went hurling on, till he came down, *flump*, on the shore of his native country.

And on the shore of his native country he sat and gaped, like one who had lost his wits.

What to do now? It was no good trying to go back to the Kingdom of Ocean; he didn't know the way there. And even had he known the way, it was too far off. So he got up and tramped across country till he came to the village where he was born.

His father and mother rejoiced to see him, for they had believed him drowned. They supposed that now he would be going to join another ship?

Join another ship! Not he! He had had enough of the ocean forever and a day!

Then how would he live?

Well, he still had in his pocket the jewels he had plucked from the trees on the island. So he sold them and bought a little farm. And by and by he fell in love with a girl in the village. He told her all about the mermaid; but she didn't seem to think that a thing with a tail mattered one way or the other. So they got married.

Sometimes the sailor remembered the time when he had been a king, and then he would think rather longingly of his queen under the ocean. But he thought of her less and less as the years passed, and he lived happily enough with his new wife.

But whether his mermaid queen still thought of him, or whether she didn't—who can tell?

6

Margrette

Once upon a time there was a beautiful girl called Margrette, who went down to the shore to gather shells. And as she walked by the edge of the water, an old merman king looked up at her out of a wave.

'Oh ho ho!' thought the merman king, 'that little beauty would make me a pretty pet!'

So he washed his wave over her, and carried her down to his palace at the bottom of the sea. It was a wonderful palace, finer than any palace ever seen on earth; but, all the same, Margrette cried when she got there.

'What are you crying for?' asked the merman king.

'I want to go home,' said she.

'No, you can't go home,' said he. 'I'm going to keep you for a pet. I've never owned a pet before, and I've always wanted one. Now, stop crying, do—I'm not going to eat you!'

The merman king was very proud of his new pet. He kept her in a coral grot, and summoned all his courtiers to admire her.

'Come and look at my little earth creature!' he said. 'Isn't she charming?'

And the courtiers said, 'Wonderfully charming!' though secretly they thought the king was being rather silly.

'She wants to go home,' said the king. 'But I shan't let her—well, would you?'

And the courtiers said, 'Oh no, certainly not! *Go home!* What an idea!'

Now the king had a son, who was handsome as handsome; and he had been away on his travels, visiting the kingdoms of the other monarchs of ocean. He came home early one morning, having travelled all night. He wanted to have his breakfast, and he wanted to rest; but the king wouldn't let him do one or the other until he had taken him to the coral grot to see his new pet.

And when the prince saw Margrette—what happened? He fell in love with her there and then. Now he didn't want his breakfast, and he didn't want to go and rest. All he wanted was to stay where he was and look at her. And as for Margrette, she fell in love with the prince, just as quickly. So there they were gazing at each other, and falling deeper in love every moment.

'Well, my son,' said the merman king. 'What do you make of her? A rare prize—don't you agree?'

The prince didn't answer. What was his father thinking of? Showing off this wonderful girl as if she were just some strange sort of animal! The prince turned hot with shame; and tears came into his eyes.

Then tears came into Margrette's eyes, too. And they neither of them said anything, but just gazed at one another.

But later that morning, when the king was busy with his councillors, the prince went back to the coral grot and took Margrette's hand.

'I love you,' he said. 'And I think you love me?'

'I love you with all my heart,' said Margrette.

'Then will you be my wife?' asked the prince.

'Your father will never permit it,' said Margrette sadly.

'My father must and shall!' said the prince.

That day, when the king and the prince sat at dinner together, the prince couldn't eat a thing. First he smiled, then he sighed, then he smiled again. The king got irritable, and said, 'What's the matter with you that you behave like an idiot?'

'Father,' said the prince, 'I wish to ask your permission to marry.'

'Well, you have my permission,' said the king. 'I've settled all that whilst you've been away. You are to marry the daughter of the king of the outer ocean. She's no beauty, and I hear she has a bad temper; but the alliance will unite our two kingdoms, and that will be a great thing.'

'I do not wish to marry the daughter of the king of the outer ocean,' said the prince. 'I wish to marry Margrette.'

'*What!*' cried the king, and he burst out laughing. 'Marry a little earth creature! My dear son, what are you thinking of? Why, she hasn't even got a tail!'

'I love her,' said the prince. 'I will marry no one else.'

The king said, 'You will do as I tell you. You will marry the daughter of the king of the outer ocean.'

The prince said, 'I will not!'

The king said, 'You will!'

The prince said, 'You shall kill me first!'

The king said 'I won't kill *you*. But it looks as if I shall have to kill that little earth creature. Oh what a pity! Such dear little feet! But there, I can have her embalmed, I suppose, and kept in a crystal case. I don't want to do it! How tiresome you are! The very first pet that ever I had, and now I've got to destroy her!'

'No, no!' cried the prince. 'Rather than that, I will marry whom you please.'

'Now I call that sensible,' said the king. 'And the little earth creature shall be chief bridesmaid, and hold a candle behind the bride's chair at the betrothal feast. Yes, that will be original and pretty. Now cheer up, like a good lad!'

Of course the prince didn't cheer up. He felt desperate. The king hurried on the preparations for the wedding; and when the bride arrived, the prince felt more desperate than ever. She was hideous, with sea weed for hair, and yellow eyes, and webbed fingers, and a purple tail. She was so hideous that the prince gave a shout of laughter when he saw her.

'What are you laughing at?' said she.

'At you! At you!' cried the prince.

'You may laugh now,' said the bride; 'but I'll make you weep when you've married me!'

'I will never marry you!' said the prince.

'You will! You will!' said the bride.

And, 'You will! You will!' said the king.

The prince went on laughing. He couldn't stop. He was crying really, you see; but it came out of him in laughter.

They sat down to the betrothal feast. Margrette stood behind the bride's chair with a lighted candle in her hand. The prince wouldn't look at the bride: he turned his head and looked at Margrette. Margrette looked at the prince, and the candle shook in her hand.

The bride said, 'Take that nasty creature away! She'll drip grease over me!'

The king said, 'If she does, I'll cut off her head!'

He laid his sword on the table. He was chuckling. He had no intention of cutting off Margrette's head. He thought it all very funny.

The candle in Margrette's hand shook and shook; and the grease went drip, drip, drip.

A spot of grease fell on the bride's neck, and she jumped up with a scream.

'Oh, oh, cut off her head, or I won't stay here another minute!'

The king said, 'I don't want to cut off her head. She's my little pet. Sit down and be sensible!'

The bride screamed, 'I won't sit down!'

And she turned and gave Margrette a slap in the face.

Then the prince got up, took the bride by her shoulders and shook her till her seaweedy hair fell off. It was only a wig, and she looked so queer without it that the king laughed outright.

'I won't stay here to be insulted!' shrieked the bride. 'I'm off! I'm off!'

She was in a rare rage, as well she might be! She dashed out, got into her silver chariot, and whipped up her team of sea horses. Away she went, back to the outer ocean, with a great train of sword fishes and jelly fishes swimming before and behind her.

The king couldn't stop laughing. Neither could the prince. He was laughing for joy now. He blew out the candle and took Margrette in his arms; and then she laughed also, though she had been shedding bitter tears.

'Dear me!' said the king. 'I see you were right, my son. That bald-headed hag was no bride for you. But we can't waste this good feast. So I suppose you must marry your little earth creature. Come to think of it, she can still be my little pet. So now everything is well. And we can all be happy.'

Margrette and the prince were married, and they were happy. But all was not quite well. And that was the king's doing. For he gave Margrette a magic mirror for a wedding present, and by turning the mirror about, you could see everything that was going on in the world, both under the water and above it. So, one day, when Margrette was turning the mirror about and about, she chanced to turn it on her home; and there she saw her mother weeping, and her father trying to comfort her mother, and her brother and sister with such grave, grave faces, and her little pet dog with his ears down, crouched at their feet and whimpering.

'How could I have forgotten them all?' she thought. 'And now they must believe me drowned, and they will never be happy any more!'

Then her own face became as sorrowful as the faces in the mirror.

'What is the matter that you look so sad?' asked the prince.

Margrette said, 'I have seen my home. I have seen my people grieving for me. I would like to go and tell them that I am well and happy.'

And the prince cried out, 'Oh, my dearest wife, I beg you not to think of them! For if you remember them, you will forget me!'

'It is impossible that I should forget you!' said Margrette.

She tried not to think of her home, but the more she tried to put the thought away from her, the more it came back. She thought of her mother weeping, and then she wept herself.

The prince couldn't bear to see her unhappy.

'If you really want to visit your people, you shall go,' he said. 'But promise me two things. First, that you will return before sunset. Second, that you will let no one kiss you: for the kiss will bring forgetfulness, and you will remember me no more.'

No, no, that could never be, Margrette told him. She could never, never forget him! But she promised to let no one kiss her, and to return before sunset. And the prince swam with her to the margin of the sea, and watched her walk away up the beach to her home.

'Mother! Father! Sister! Brother!' Margrette ran in calling them.

They crowded round her, laughing and crying in their surprise and joy. They sought to embrace her, but she thrust them away.

'No, no, no one must kiss me! I have promised my husband that no one shall kiss me!'

But when she sat down, her little pet dog, who had been jumping round her and barking for joy, leaped into her lap, put up his little muzzle, and kissed her on the cheek.

For a moment Margrette sat quite still with the dog in her lap. Then she jumped up, kissed her mother, kissed her father, kissed her sister and her brother. Yes, they might embrace each other now as much as they liked. For, with the little dog's kiss, all memory of her merman prince had vanished from Margrette's mind.

And so she lived on in her home as if she had never left it. And when her people questioned her about where she had been, she shook her head and said, 'I think—I fell asleep.' And seeing that their questions troubled her, they ceased to ask her anything. They were only too glad to have her safely home.

'She has grown more beautiful whilst she was away, wherever she's been,' said her mother.

That was true. She was so radiantly beautiful that to look on her was to love her. Many and many a man came seeking her in marriage; and though she refused them all, she didn't know why.

But one night she couldn't sleep. The tide was full: she could hear the waves breaking on the beach, and it seemed to her that the waves were moaning.

'Why are they so sad?' she said to herself.

'Margrette! Margrette!' Surely the waves were calling her name? She listened. No, they were not calling anything; they were just breaking on the beach... But then—yes, there they were calling again, 'Margrette! Margrette!'

She fell asleep at last. But in her dreams the waves kept on calling.

'Margrette!' said the waves. And then a hush. And then, 'Margrette!' again.

All next day she walked on the beach, trying to remember something she had forgotten. The sun was bright, and the sea calm; the little ripples ran up against her feet, ran back: they were merely whispering. Were they whispering her name? She scarcely knew.

But that night a wind sprang up, and the waves broke shouting on the beach. And every wave as it turned over shouted, 'Mar-*grette!*' She sat up in bed. 'Why are they calling me? Oh, *why* are they?'

The voices of the waves grew louder and louder. It was not only her name they were calling now. 'Margrette! *Margrette!*' they called. 'Oh I have waited so long, so long! And still you do not come! I am so lonely, Margrette—Margrette, my darling! So—lonely!'

She leaped from her bed and ran down to the beach.

'*Margrette! Margrette! Margrette!*' Earth, sea and sky were clamorous with her name. The night was pitchy dark, but memory flooded back into her mind and lightened it. How could she ever have forgotten her merman prince? How could she? She threw herself into the sea, and his arms were round her.

Together they sank under the waves. And under the waves they lived happily ever after.

7

Long John and the Mermaid

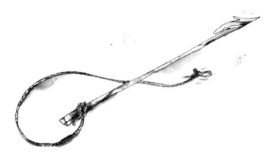

Once upon a time there was a foolish little mermaid who lived near an island, and she fell in love with a whale. Long John was the whale's name.

The little mermaid's father said, 'My dear child, do be sensible! A whale is no fit husband for you.'

And the little mermaid's mother said, 'You ought to be ashamed of yourself, making eyes at Long John! Where's your pride? Any one can see he doesn't care twopence about you!'

And that was true; he didn't. But there she was, always chasing after him between the island and the mainland, and offering him kelp cakes and fish pies.

Long John took the kelp cakes and the fish pies; and when he had eaten them, he blew bubbles at her, gave a flick of his great tail, and with a wink of his little eye, and a chuckle in his fat throat—*woosh!* down he dived under the island and came up laughing on the far side.

'Give me a ride on your back, Long John!' cried the little mermaid, swimming round the island after him.

But—*woosh!* down went Long John under the island again, and came up laughing and blowing bubbles on the near side.

So then the little mermaid made a green-weed harness to bridle Long John. But he wouldn't stop still to be bridled; so she bribed all the crabs and lobsters that lived in the island pools to sit on Long John's tail and hold him still. But when the crabs and lobsters had crowded on to his tail, Long John set off through the sea at a tremendous pace, turning and twisting and threshing his tail about. The crabs and lobsters got giddy; they fell off one after the other, and had to walk all the way back to the island. They were very angry, and told the little mermaid just what they thought of her. And that made her cry.

Then she made up doleful songs about Long John and how much she loved him; and she sang those songs night and day. And what with her singing and her howling, she made herself such a nuisance that all the other mermaids and the crabs and the lobsters and the fishes and everything that lived in the sea kept out of her way. And she was very lonely.

So by and by she got so that she didn't love Long John any more— she hated him. But love him, or hate him, it made no difference to Long John; he went on blowing bubbles and chuckling whenever he met her.

There was only one person in the sea or on the land that Long John respected, and that was the great whale hunter, Ichabod Paddock, who lived on the coast opposite the island. Ichabod Paddock had been the death of many a great whale; and though he hadn't been the death of Long John yet, still, Long John had a shuddery feeling down his spine that one day he might be.

So when the foolish little mermaid began to hate Long John and wanted her revenge on him, she thought of Ichabod Paddock.

One quiet evening, Ichabod was sitting on a rock by the sea, smoking his pipe and thinking his thoughts, when he heard a *ripple*, *ripple*, and saw a silvery sparkle on the calm water; and then he saw a gleaming head and a white arm, and there was the little mermaid hailing him.

Said Ichabod, 'How d'you do?'

Said the mermaid, 'Evening, Ichabod! Do you see what I'm holding in my hand?'

'Looks like a rope of pearls,' said Ichabod.

'It *is* a rope of pearls,' said the little mermaid. 'It's a gift to the man who will kill Long John. And will that man be you, Ichabod?'

'I don't care about pearls, myself,' said Ichabod.

'Then diamonds?'

'Don't care much about diamonds, either.'

'Then a chest full of treasure?'

'I'm not that greedy.'

'Then my love?'

'Now don't be silly,' said Ichabod. 'I'll own you're pretty. But what should I do with a wife that's got a tail?'

'Then what *will* move you?'

'Nothing, that I knows of,' said Ichabod.

'Then I think you're horrid,' said the little mermaid. 'And I'll haunt you day and night!'

She did, too. She used to climb up the rocks and sit under his bedroom window, and howl doleful songs all night; and when he was at sea she got under the boat and rocked it so that it nearly foundered.

And she became such a nuisance that one day Ichabod said: 'Now see here, my girl, I'm a peaceable man, and I like my quiet. So you can take a message to Long John from me. Tell him that Ichabod Paddock will never draw harpoon against him, if so be as he'll let you bridle him and ride you once round the Great Cape.' The Great Cape was the promontory on which Ichabod Paddock lived.

The little mermaid was delighted. She swam off to find Long John and give him Ichabod's message. She thought that once she got the bridle on him, she could do what she liked with him.

And Long John was delighted too, for now he thought he need never get that shivery feeling down his spine again.

So Long John let the little mermaid put her green-weed bridle on him, and she climbed on to his head and sat there in triumph, with her green hair rippling and her silver scales all a-glitter. The crabs and lobsters crowded round to watch. Long John gave them a wink, and off he went.

Up along the coast he swam, tame as any shrimp; and now and then he tacked, pretending he was a frigate. The little mermaid sang happy songs, and told Long John to join in the chorus, but he wouldn't. He said he must save his breath for swimming and blowing bubbles. They were rainbow bubbles he blew; the bubbles were floating round them in showers all along the surface of the waves, and the little mermaid laughed and said, 'How pretty!'

So there they were tacking round the Great Cape, and Ichabod Paddock was standing on a cliff to watch them. He could see the little mermaid's green hair waving like a flag in the breeze, and her silver scales glittering, and Long John's great mouth agrin, and his little eyes winking. And the rainbow bubbles were floating up and breaking against Ichabod's knees.

And then he saw Long John make a tack way out to sea, and turn, and take a dive to swim under water. And under water he came swimmimg straight towards shore again. And when he was close in shore, up he came—AND SPOUTED.

Up, up, up, went the spout, and up, up, up astride of it went the little mermaid. She lost her grip of the green-weed bridle, she went sailing over the land higher and higher and farther and farther from the sea. Over the cliffs she sailed, and over the dunes, and over the roofs of a little town. The people looked up and saw the whole sky above them a-glitter with that water spout, and on top of the spout they saw what looked like a silver splinter. And then—'Mind your heads!' for the water spout was coming down again. Some of it fell in rain over the town, but the most of it sailed on and fell into a great lake.

Splash! The little mermaid fell into the lake; and down she went, and down to the very bottom.

And in that lake the little mermaid had to stay; for you can't walk far on a tail, and no one came to carry her back over land to the sea. Nobody wanted her back, that was the truth of it. They left her to sing her doleful songs to the sun and the moon and the stars, who were too busy shining to bother about her.

As to Long John, he gave a wink to Ichabod Paddock and swam back to the island. The crabs and lobsters helped him off with the green-weed bridle, and tore it to pieces with their claws.

Ichabod Paddock watched the broken bits of the bridle washing about in the tide, and said, 'She thought to go whale-riding, but she went sky-riding instead. Oh, what a foolish little mermaid!'

But Long John couldn't help feeling just a bit grateful to her; because after all, he was safe forever now from Ichabod's harpoon.

8

The Magical Tune

Y ou must know that there once lived in Ireland a blind piper called Maurice Connor. To be sure, there were many pretty pipers in Ireland then; but they all had to own themselves beaten when Maurice tuned up. His tunes could make you sing, they could make you laugh, they could make you cry; and there was one magical tune he had that made you dance, whether you would or no. As soon as he struck up that tune, off you whisked like a straw in a storm: there was no stopping whilst that tune lasted. It made you dance the shoes off your feet; and still, as long as he played, you must go on dancing. Where Maurice learned that tune, nobody knew; he kept the secret to himself. And he didn't play it very often, which was just as well, or there wouldn't have been a decent pair of shoes left on anybody's feet in all the countryside.

Maurice had a good old mother, and since he couldn't see, she used to lead him about from one place to another, wherever people were gathered together, and wanted a piper to help them make merry. Of course, Maurice had scores of good dance tunes, besides the magical one; and it was understood that at these gatherings he should keep off his magic tune, and give the people reels and country dances, so that they could stop when they had danced enough.

Well now, one summer holiday, there was to be a dance at Trafraska, which was a clean, smooth stretch of a sandy bay, with a sheltering background to it of rocks and cliffs. It was a fine morning, and all was peaceful in Trafraska Bay, with the little waves just turning over with a gentle *slap, slap.*

There was a great crowd of people gathered, both old and young, all in their holiday best. Mrs Connor (she that was Maurice's mother) led Maurice down amongst them, and put him to sit on a little rock. So there he sat and played one merry tune after another; and the young danced, and the old looked on, till it came dinner time, and then they all sat about on the sand and ate what they had brought in their baskets.

After that, Maurice thought it was time to go home. But not a bit of it! They must dance again! And dance they did till tea time, with Maurice puffing out his cheeks and going at it with the pipes, now fast, now slow, now merry, now languishing, till he was fairly tired of the whole concern.

'I'm finished now,' he said, and made to get off his rock.

But, 'One more tune, Maurice, just one more tune!' they all shouted.

So he played them one more tune, and they danced one more dance;

and if Maurice thought that was to be the last of it, it wasn't. They must have another dance and yet another, till it seemed to Maurice that they meant to keep him there all night.

So he got vexed. 'Well then, be jabbers, if you want to dance all night—here's for you!' cried he. And he drew a deep breath, and—Heaven save us!—out he blasted his magical tune.

What happened after that was a thing to marvel at. There was all that crowd of people, old and young—babies, grannies, grandads and all—leaping and jigging and whirling and twirling as if they'd taken leave of their senses. Maurice himself couldn't keep still; he was off his rock and prancing about as madly as any one. And as for his mother, she had her skirts gathered up in her two hands, and she was high in the air and down again, and up again, and round and round on her skinny old legs like any slip of a girl.

But old Mrs Connor's dancing, yes, and the dancing of all the rest, was nothing to what was happening farther down the sands. For out of the sea every manner of creature came jumping and plunging, till every inch of the sands that wasn't covered by people's dancing feet was covered with dancing fishes.

Crabs and lobsters of monstrous size were spinning round and round on one claw; herds of seals came galloping out of the waves to join in the fun; scallops and oysters leaped up and down, clapping their shells together like castanets; rainbow-coloured mackerel, herrings in silver showers, cod, halibut, John Dories, sprats, turbot, sharks—there wasn't a fish you could name that wasn't bounding out of the sea to join in the dance. Never was such a dance seen, never such a hullabaloo heard, since time began.

The people were crying on Maurice to stop; but not he! It seemed as if he couldn't stop. And all the time that he was playing, he was whirling round as crazily as the best of them. And as to shoes—soon there wasn't a whole shoe left anywhere.

Well, at the height of all these doings, what should come dancing out of the sea but a most beautiful young mermaid. She wore a little hat cocked on the side of her head, and the hair that streamed down from under it was just the colour of the green sea in the shallows when the sunlight runs through it. As to her coral lips and her pearly teeth, her deep blue eyes, and all the rest of it—nothing so lovely had ever been seen on that beach before. And up she came dancing on her little silvery tail to Maurice. And though he, poor thing, being blind, couldn't see the loveliness of her, yet he heard her voice singing, and it was sweet as honey:

> 'I'm a lady of honour
> Who lives in the sea;
> Come down, Maurice Connor,
> And be married to me.
> Silver plate and gold dishes
> You shall have, and shall be
> The king of the fishes
> When you're married to me.'

Well, well, Maurice wasn't going to be outdone at rhyming, nor at singing, either. So, still dancing, and still playing, he sang out (and it was clever of him, surely, to sing and pipe at the same time, but he managed it), so:

'I'm obliged to you, madam.
Off a gold dish or plate,
If a king, and I had 'em,
I could dine in great state.
With your own father's daughter
I'd be sure to agree,
But to drink the salt water
Would not do for me!'

'Oh then, Maurice,' said she, twirling round and round him, 'isn't it yourself that's a fine poet? And that's another reason why I should love you!'

And she caught him by the elbow, and they danced, and danced, and danced, Maurice being by this time scared to stop playing, because with so many big sharks about, not to mention crabs and lobsters and seals, all of them enjoying the dance, he wasn't sure what they might do to him, if he vexed them by breaking off his tune.

That mermaid fairly danced him down to the edge of the water, all the time coaxing him with her pretty speeches, and telling him he'd no need to be afraid of the salt water, as he'd find plenty of other nice things to drink down in the ocean. And as for any fear he might have of drowning, she had a little cocked hat for him just like her own, and with that on his head he could live as comfortably under the sea as on land.

'It's a king you'll be, my darling,' she said. 'And then there's your sight. I've got a medicine in my golden casket at home will put that right for you.'

Well, that decided Maurice in a trice: to get his sight, and to be a king into the bargain—what more could any man in his senses ask? So then said he, 'I'll come.'

But when his old mother saw him and the mermaid prancing off into the shallow water through the thick of the fishes, and he still playing, she let out a screech that made the cliffs ring. And there she was, leaping about on her old skinny legs, and fair galloping after him, crying on him to come back.

'Oh, then,' she wailed, 'if I wasn't widow enough before, but he must be going off from me to be married to that unnatural creature! And who knows but 'tis grandmother I may be to a hake or a cod— heaven help and pity me!—and maybe 'tis boiling and eating my own grandchild I'll be, with a bit of salt butter, and I not knowing it! Oh Maurice, Maurice, if there's any nature left in you at all, come back to your old mother, who's kept you safe as her own pet lamb from the hour you were born to this very day!'

But Maurice went on dancing in the shallow water and playing his magical tune, with the mermaid holding him by the elbow and drawing him farther in. And there was a big thundering wave coming, as if it meant to swallow him alive. Maurice couldn't see it, and so he didn't fear it, but his old mother saw it, even through the tears that were gushing out of her eyes. And yet, tears, heartache, terror and all, for the life of her she couldn't stop her old bones from skipping and frisking, because Maurice never stopped playing that tune on the pipes.

Botheration! The commotion his mother was making threatened to put Maurice out in his tune; so he just paused long enough to call out, 'Whisht with you, mammy, me darling! Sure, I'm going to be king over the fishes down in the sea, and to get my sight, and all! And for a token that I'm well and happy, I'll send you, every twelve month on this day, a piece of burnt wood to Trafraska beach.'

That was all he had time to say; for the mermaid, seeing the great thundering wave just upon them, covered him up with herself in a thing like a cloak with a big hood to it. Then the wave curled over the two of them, twice the height of their heads, and burst upon the sands with such a rush and a roar as completely snuffed out the sound of poor Mrs Connor's wailing voice.

When the wave went back, there wasn't a fish, nor a crab, nor a lobster, nor a seal, nor an oyster to be seen on all that beach. Everything was quiet: the limpets were back on the rocks; and as to the crowds of people, the dance went out of their legs, and they just fell down, and lay where they fell, till they got their breath and their strength back, and were able to hobble to their homes.

Maurice's mother had to go home with the rest. She got used to living alone in time; and, sure enough, on a twelve month to that day, a piece of burnt wood washed up for her on Trafraska beach. She took the piece of wood back to her cottage, and hung it over the chimney place. And every year, on the same date, there came another piece for her, till her kitchen was fair loaded with them. So she knew Maurice was alive and happy; and if he had got his sight back—well, wasn't that something any mother should be thankful for?

People say that those pieces of wood came washing in regularly at the appointed time for the next hundred years. They say, too, that the men who went out in boats on still evenings could often hear the

77

sound of music coming up through the water. And some, who were extra sharp of hearing, could plainly hear Maurice's voice singing away down there to the tune of his pipes.

And this was his song:

> 'Beautiful shore, with thy spreading strand,
> Thy crystal water and diamond sand,
> Never would I have parted with thee,
> But for the sake of my fair lady.'

9

The Comb, the Flute and the Spinning Wheel

Once upon a time there was a merchant who traded over seas. For a time he prospered, but then things went wrong with him: his ships foundered, his clients cheated him, and he became very poor. He didn't know what to do; he felt desperate. He lay awake all night, and by day he wandered about tearing his hair like a man gone crazed.

One day he was walking up and down by a creek of the sea, moaning and wondering whether the best thing for him to do wouldn't be to jump in and drown himself, when a mermaid spoke to him out of a wave. 'Merchant, merchant,' said she, 'why do you go about tearing your hair and wailing? All my waves are crying out because of your misery.'

'I am ruined! I am ruined!' cried he. And he told her all that had happened.

Said the mermaid, 'If you will give me just one little thing that I lack, I will make you richer and more prosperous than you have ever been.'

'I will give you anything!' said the merchant.

'The youngest thing in your house, that is all I lack,' said the mermaid.

The merchant remembered that in his house was a greyhound bitch with a litter of puppies, not more than three days old. The mermaid could have the latest born of these puppies and welcome! So he gave her his promise. She sank down under the wave again, and the merchant went home full of joy.

But when he came to the gate of his house, a servant ran out to greet him with the news that his wife had just given birth to a baby boy. Then the merchant tore his hair again, and rushed to his wife, to tell her of his terrible promise. But she comforted him and said, 'We will never let our little son go near the sea, and then the mermaid cannot take him.'

The mermaid kept her part of the bargain. Ships that the merchant believed to have foundered came home laden with gold; those men who had cheated him repented, and paid him what they owed; he became rich once more, richer than he had ever been. Everything prospered with him; and as the years passed, and nothing more was seen of the mermaid, he lost his dread of the promise he had made.

The baby, whom they named Stefan, grew up into a handsome lad. And since the shore was forbidden him, he took to hunting in the woods; and by and by the king of the country, seeing how bold and skilful Stefan was, took him into service as his chief huntsman. And so greatly did Stefan please that by and by the king gave him his only daughter in marriage.

Stefan and his princess lived happily together. But one day, when Stefan was hunting in the forest, a hare sprang up at his feet and doubled away out of the woods into the open fields. Stefan followed the hare, and it gave him a chase, till at last there it was bounding away from him on to the sea shore. And then it vanished.

Stefan looked about him in bewilderment. Not a trace of that hare could he see; and being hot and weary he stooped to lave his hands and face in the tranquil water. But no sooner had he touched the water than a great wave towered up and came washing in to shore. In the wave was the mermaid; and she seized Stefan in her wet arms and dragged him down with her under the sea.

When Stefan did not come home that night, the princess grew very anxious; and as soon as dawn broke, she sent out servants to search for him. They searched high and low, but they didn't find him; only, when they had searched woods and fields, and at last came to the sea shore, they saw his game bag drifting in the shallow water. And drawing it out of the water, they took it back and showed it to the princess.

Then the princess guessed what had happened, and herself ran to the sea shore. Crying bitterly, she walked up and down on the edge of the sea, calling and calling. But no one answered her.

So at last, quite worn out, she lay down on the sand and fell asleep. And in her sleep she dreamed that she was walking through a flowery meadow and came to a hut. And in the hut she found an old woman who promised to get Stefan back for her. 'I will find that old woman!' she said to herself, when she woke up.

So she set out to look for the flowery meadow, and many a weary day she wandered without finding it. But at last just when she was in despair and thinking of turning home again—there was the flowery meadow right in front of her, with the little hut at the far end of it. She ran across the meadow and knocked at the door of the hut. An old, old voice bade her come in; and when she went in, there, sure enough, was the old woman, spinning by the fire.

'Welcome, my princess,' said the good old fairy, for that's what she was. 'I know why you have come. It was I who sent you the dream. Yes, yes, we must get Stefan back for you!'

Then the old fairy gave the princess a golden comb, and told her that on the night of the next full moon, she must go down to the sea shore, comb her hair with the golden comb, and then lay the comb down on the edge of the water.

'The mermaid has lost her own comb,' said the fairy, 'and she will come for yours. It may be that she will bring Stefan with her. If she does, you must seize him and drag him out of the waves. Oh, I don't promise that you will succeed. There is such a thing as try, try, try again, you know. But you will get him back in the end.'

The princess thanked the old fairy, took the golden comb and went home. The night of the full moon seemed a long time in coming; but it came at last. And the princess went down to the sea shore, and combed her hair with the golden comb. And when she had finished combing her hair, she laid the comb down on the edge of the moonlit water, and waited.

Soon she heard a rushing and a roaring: a mighty wave rushed in and swept the comb away, and in that wave the princess plainly saw the face of Stefan, gazing sorrowfully at her.

'Stefan! Stefan!' cried the princess; and she ran into the sea to take him in her arms. But the wave fell back, the face of Stefan vanished. On the sea was nothing but calm glittering water; and on the shore only a poor little princess, weeping bitter tears.

She wept and wept; she wandered and wept, not caring where she went, until at last she was so weary that she lay down and fell asleep. And in her sleep she dreamed the same dream of the flowery meadow, and the hut and the old woman who promised to get Stefan back for her. So once more she set out to find the flowery meadow, and in the end she found it, and went into the hut and told the old fairy of her bitter grief.

This time the old fairy gave her a golden flute, and told her to go down to the shore on the night of the next full moon, play on the golden flute, and then lay it down on the edge of the water.

So the princess took the flute and went home and waited till the moon was full again, and a weary time that waiting seemed to her. But at last the night of the full moon came, and with it came a wind and clouds that raced over the face of the moon; and the wind flung the sea about into thousands of leaping and sparkling waves.

The princess stood by the sea and played on the golden flute; and the tune that she played was loud and clear and full of longing. Then she put the flute down on the edge of the waves.

Soon she heard a rushing and a roaring; the leaping waves gathered themselves into one huge wave, and the huge wave came swiftly in and swept the flute away. And in the wave the princess plainly saw the head of Stefan. The head rose up higher and higher, till Stefan was half above the water, and the princess rushed into the sea to clasp him in her arms. But the huge wave rolled her over, and blinded her with spray; and when it drew back, it swept Stefan away with it.

There she was now, standing alone on the shore, under the moon and the hurrying clouds, by the leaping and sparkling water.

Again she wandered until she was utterly weary, again she lay down and slept, again she dreamed of the flowery meadow and the hut and the old fairy who promised to get Stefan back for her. Again she found the old fairy, and besought her help.

The old fairy gave her a golden spinning wheel, and told her to go down to the shore on the night of the next full moon and spin, and then to leave the spinning wheel on the edge of the water.

So the princess went home with the spinning wheel, and waited.

And when the night of the full moon came, the wind howled, and black storm clouds toppled across the sky, with the moon brightening, and vanishing, and brightening again among them. The princess staggered with the golden spinning wheel down to the shore; and there she sat and span, whilst the spinning wheel rocked in the wind, and the sea roared, and the great waves pounded on the beach. But still the princess sat and span; and when her thread was finished, she laid the spinning wheel down on the edge of the breakers, and waited.

Then all the breakers gathered themselves into one huge wave, and in that wave the princess saw Stefan holding out his arms to her.

In under the curling and foaming crest of that wave she rushed, and caught Stefan by the hands: the wave roared and beat upon her, but still she held tight to Stefan's hands; the wave lifted her off her feet and flung her here and there, but still she held tight; the wave whirled her high into the air, but still she held tight. And then, with a mighty roar, the wave broke upon the beach and washed away the spinning wheel; and when it ran back—there were Stefan and the princess standing on the shore, clasped in each other's arms.

But only for a moment. There came a voice from far out over the water, a mocking voice that cried out, 'If I cannot keep him, neither shall you!' And another huge wave came racing in, and drew them out, and tore them apart, and left them struggling in the water.

'Stefan! Stefan!' 'My princess! My princess!'

They called wildly to each other, but neither could reach the other, and neither could reach the shore. And the waves drew them under and beat the breath out of them.

Then in her despair the princess thought of the good old fairy, and cried on her to help them. And the good old fairy heard, and in a moment Stefan was changed into a gleaming mackerel, and the princess into a silver herring. There they were now, swimming safely under the waves, but not together, nor could they find each other. The sea bore them farther and farther apart, and tossed them up on land at last, in a strange country.

As soon as the mackerel touched the shore, it turned into Stefan again. As soon as the herring touched the shore, it turned into the princess. But a great stretch of farmland and pasture land and woodland lay between them. To earn a livelihood, Stefan in his part of the country became a shepherd; and the princess in her part of the country became a shepherdess. And so for many years they herded their flocks in solitude and sadness.

And after many years, the shepherd, herding his flocks to fresher pastures, came to that part of the country where the shepherdess was living. And they met, and became friends, but they did not recognise each other.

But one evening, when the moon was full and they were watching their flocks together, the shepherd took up his pipe and began to play. The tune he played was loud and clear and full of longing. It made the shepherdess think of the night when she had sat on the shore and played on the golden flute. And she burst into tears.

'Why do you weep?' said the shepherd.

'I weep because my memories are sad,' she answered.

'Tell me your memories,' said the shepherd.

At first she would not; but at last she did. And in the telling of that tale they knew each other again.

'You are my princess!' cried Stefan.

'And you are my Stefan!' cried she.

So they sold their flocks, and took ship, and returned joyfully to their own country.

The king had been mourning for the loss of his daughter; the merchant and his wife had been mourning for the loss of their son. Now they all rejoiced and made merry together. The mermaid never troubled them again: she knew herself beaten. And so they all lived in peace and happiness ever after.

The Magic Lake

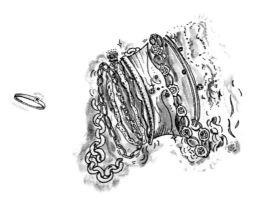

Well, well, there was a lake with a bad name. Many a man had gone to swim in it. It seemed to be coaxing people into it, that lake did, so cool and clear its waters looked on a hot summer's day. But of all the young fellows who went swimming there, not one returned. They just vanished. So by and by nobody went to swim in it any more.

Now there was a young farmer called Rory Keating, and he was going to be married. So he went into town to buy a wedding ring for his girl. And his way, both going and coming, led past this lake. In the town he met up with some friends, and they all set out to walk home together. Rory was in wild spirits, and his comrades not much less so. They got larking as they walked along, and every now and then Rory would take the ring out of his pocket and twirl it up against the sun.

Oh dear, he did that once too often; for as they were coming along by the lake, and he twirling that ring up, the ring gave a jump and fell into the water. It gave a little twinkle as it struck the water; and then it vanished. Of course it did; it sank down to the bottom—if that lake had any bottom. Anyway, the ring disappeared.

Rory was in a fine distraction: he thought of jumping in after the ring; but then he thought better of it. He remembered all the young fellows who had jumped in and been seen no more. And if that happened to him—what would his Peggy do? She would fade away and die of grief: yes, surely she would.

But there were other young fellows with him who hadn't any particular sweethearts; so he called out, 'Five guineas to the man who'll dive in and bring up my ring!'

But no one would dive in. They weren't such fools.

So, as they were standing there, wondering what to do, Rory urging one man after another to dive, and all of them making excuses, up came a lad called Padeen, whose wits weren't as bright as they might have been: at least that's what people thought.

'What's going on with the crowd of ye?' said Padeen.

So they told him. And he said, 'Is that heaven's truth, that there's five golden guineas going for the man who gets that ring?'

'Aye, it's heaven's truth,' said Rory. 'See, here they are, the five bright yellow boys!' And he held out his hand, and there were the five guineas plain to see in his palm.

'Then it's myself is the man for the attempt!' said Padeen.

And into the lake he dived, just as he was, jacket, boots, and all.

He was going, going, going, down and down and down, till his lungs felt like bursting. There seemed to be no bottom to that lake. And then, all of a sudden, the water parted from around him, and there he was, standing on dry ground. There was a bright blue sky over his head, and there was a broad path under his feet. And he walked along that path till he came to a gate. In through the gate he went, and found himself in fine pleasure grounds, with an elegant avenue winding through them. And in those pleasure grounds there were scores of gardeners working; and when Padeen looked at those gardeners he saw familiar faces; for whose were those faces but the faces of the young fellows who had gone to swim in the lake from time to time, and had one and all disappeared.

So Padeen was walking along, hailing one or the other, with 'Hullo, Jack O'Toole!' and 'A pleasure, I'm sure, to see you, Ned Flannagan!' and 'The top of the morning to ye, Billy Doody!'—all that sort of thing. But not a man of them so much as gave him a look. They worked away, digging, and planting, and weeding, and spreading gravel on the little side paths. And as they were working, they were singing:

> 'Fair her face, and white her skin—
> Have you courage her to win?
> And her wealth it far outshines
> Afric's gold and silver mines.
> She exceeds all heart can wish,
> Neither rude nor tigerish,
> But sweet as roses in a bower,
> And graceful as the lily flower.'

That song made Padeen hurry his steps; for he was all stirred up, now, to make the acquaintance of the beautiful maiden they were singing about.

So he came at last to a grand house, with a grand flight of steps going up to the front door. And seeing that the door was open, he made so bold as to go in.

'Any one home?'

And—would you believe it?—out from the kitchen came flip-flapping the fattest and ugliest mermaid that ever man saw. She had pig's eyes and wolf's teeth, and the great mouth that was on her was grinning from ear to ear. The greeny white hair hung about her head like lichen on an old tree, and she was all decked about with heavy gold chains and bracelets that jangled as she came.

'Good morning, Padeen,' said she.

'Good morning, ma'am,' said he. 'Though maybe it's evening, after all.'

'And what brought you here?' said she. 'Wasn't it for love of me you came?' And the giggle she let out of her when she said that shook and wrinkled her fat cheeks so's they made Padeen think of boiling gruel.

'Well, ma'am,' said he, 'first and foremost I'm come after Rory Keating's gold ring.'

'I have it in my hand,' said she.

And she gave it to him.

'Thank you, ma'am,' said he. 'I needn't say may your shadow never grow less, for it's a powerful one enough already. But I wish you all the good in the world. And so will you tell me, please, ma'am, how I am to get out of here? Do I return the way I came?'

'Oh! Oh!' said she, flying into a rage. 'I thought you had come to marry me!'

'Now don't you go and upset yourself, my darling,' said Padeen. 'You must wait till I come back again. I'm to be paid for this errand, so go I must with the ring, or they'll all be wondering what's keeping me.'

'Never mind about the dratted money!' said she. 'If you marry me you shall live in this house for ever, and want for nothing.'

'And have you had many husbands, ma'am?' said he, just to keep her in humour. (He was all the time edging back to the door, and she flapping after him.)

'Well, a good few offers,' said she. 'But they didn't please me, so I set them to till the pleasure grounds. Maybe you caught sight of them as you came along?'

'I saw one or two,' said Padeen. 'And weren't they singing your praises!'

'Ah, if they didn't do that, they'd get no supper,' said she. 'Looks such as mine must be flattered, you know.'

'You're right about that, ma'am,' said Padeen, going edgeways down the steps, and keeping his eye on her.

'Well then, why call me ma'am?' said she. 'Aren't I your darling, Padeen?'

So he called her his darling, and all the pretty names he could think of, whilst getting back along the avenue best way he could: she puffing and flapping along after him, and the song from the gardeners dinning his ears, for they struck up extra loud when they saw her.

Well, they came to the gate at the end of the avenue, and Padeen nipped through and shut it after him. And there was the water all about him again.

Up he plunged through the water, and up and up, and looking round all the time to see was the mermaid following him. But, praise be, there wasn't a sight of her. Indeed, what with her fat, and the weight of her bracelets and chains, she was fair winded by the time she had followed him as far as the gate. She could only stand at the gate and screech up after him, 'Come back, my Padeen, come back quickly!'

So up with him through the water, and up and up, till he broke surface. And weren't Rory Keating and the rest of them surprised when they saw him swimming across to them from the other side of the lake!

They had just about given up their hopes of seeing him again, you understand; and yet Rory had been unwilling to leave the place, because of his ring.

'And here your ring is,' said Padeen, when he made shore. 'And I've earned my five guineas if ever man did; for she that's down below is worse than a nightmare.'

Well, well, Padeen got his five guineas, and they all looked on him with more respect after that. He thought whether he ought to go down below again, having given a kind of promise. But then he thought once more; and he came to the decision that he needn't go; because the fat mermaid had plenty of young men to choose from down there, if so be as she really wanted to marry.

The Untidy Mermaid

There was once a young farmer who lived by the sea; and in the evening, when his work was done, he would take his boat and go fishing.

So there he was, one evening, slowly rowing in the pearly twilight on a calm sea, with his fishing lines out over the stern of the boat. And down under the water there was an inquisitive little mermaid; and when the shadow of the boat passed over her, she swam up to see who was in it.

The young farmer looked found and what did he see? The most beautiful little creature he had ever set eyes on, with her white arms resting along the gunwale, and her long golden hair dripping over her gleaming shoulders, and her great green eyes gazing up at him.

And gazing up, what did the little mermaid see? The handsomest young man ever you can imagine, but with a look of stubborn pride about him, for all that.

Said the farmer, 'Good evening, my lady!'

'Oh!' said she.

And 'oh' was all she could say; for it hadn't taken her one half second to fall in love with that handsome young man, and she was struck speechless. So she let go her hold of the boat, and slipped down under the water again.

Dear me! When she went to her coral bed that night, she lay awake thinking of that young farmer; and when at last she slept, she slept dreaming of him. And next morning, as soon as the sun glimmered over the sea, there she was, perched on a rock close to the shore under his farm, combing her hair with her golden comb, and singing such heart-stirring love songs that the little waves hushed themselves to listen, and the gulls flew down in flocks and stood on the shore, quite mesmerized. But the young farmer, who was very conceited, and who thought more of himself than he should, didn't take any notice; though he heard her right enough.

So by and by her singing turned to sobbing, and the little waves sputtered with anger because of the farmer's hard heart; and the gulls clapped their wings and shouted 'Wa! Wa! Wa!' and flew round the farmer's head as he drove his plough over the furrows calling out, 'Shame on you, hard hearted monster!'

But the farmer only laughed and went on ploughing.

So then, since her songs couldn't move him, the little mermaid took to bringing the farmer gifts. She brought pearls and dropped them into his boat when he was out fishing; she brought rubies, she brought emeralds. But the farmer gathered them up and threw them back into the sea, and called out, 'You can keep your trash—*I* don't want it!'

And that made the little mermaid cry.

Then the other mermaids and the mermen got angry with the farmer for flouting her, and said, 'If you love him so much as all that, why don't you upset his boat and drag him under? We'll give you a storm!'

But the little mermaid loved her handsome young farmer too much to want to drag him under, or do anything that she thought he wouldn't like. Every evening when he went out fishing she got hold of the boat and drew it to the best fishing grounds, and that pleased him. 'Well, you're some use after all, young lady!' said he.

And that pleased *her*. So she began to feel a little bolder, and one evening she climbed right into the boat, and put her arms round him and said, 'I love you—oh how I love you! Give me a kiss!'

'Oh no you don't!' said he, quite angry. And he picked her up and tossed her back into the sea, with no more thought for her feelings than if she had been an unwanted conger eel that had got in among his catch by mistake.

So then at last *she* got angry: not angry enough to want to upset his boat and drag him under and drown him; but angry enough to give the boat a good rocking and himself a fright. And what with the big waves she sent pounding over the gunwale, and the dark fog she brought down all round the boat, he had the worst job in the world to get home that evening.

The next evening it was the same; and the next: as soon as he put out his boat the waves began to roar and the fog to spread; and himself to be spinning round and round in the boat as if he had come into the middle of a whirlpool. As to fish: of course he never caught another one.

Some folk began to laugh at him, too; and that hurt his pride. And other folk began to scare him with tales of young fellows who had been dragged down and drowned by mermaids out of spite.

'You'd best catch hold of her and bring her up on land,' they told him; 'or as sure as you're alive she'll have you down under!'

So one day, when she was bothering round the boat, he did catch hold of her; but when she understood he was for taking her ashore, she gave him a slap in the face, and leaped out of his arms as easy as easy. And so back into the sea with her.

Well, what was he to do? He took counsel of a wise woman, and the wise woman told him he hadn't gone about the right way to catch her.

'Did you notice a belt with a pouch slung to it that she was wearing?' said the wise woman. Yes, the farmer had noticed that.

'Well now,' said the wise woman; 'the pouch holds her comb and her mirror; but the belt holds her strength and her magic power. Once get hold of that belt, and she'll be like wax in your hands—you can do with her what you will.'

The farmer asked how he was to get hold of the belt; and the wise woman laughed and told him he must find out for himself. So he thought for a long time; and then he hit on the way to do it. He turned from cross to kind; he made out that he was as much in love with the little mermaid as she was with him; he flattered her, it seemed he couldn't make enough of her; he coaxed her into his boat again and took her fishing with him; he never so much as mentioned bringing her up on land; but when it was time to go home he kissed her smiling lips and eased her over the side of the boat as if she was the most precious thing in the world to him. Yes, he deceived that poor little mermaid more than any man had a right to do—though perhaps she had partly brought it on herself by being so bothering.

So one evening, when the two of them were in the boat together, with the pearly twilight round them, and the sea calm as glass, he with his arm about her, and she with her golden head on his shoulder, he said 'Comb your hair, and let me hear you sing.'

She took her comb and mirror out of the pouch, and gave him the pouch to hold; and she began to comb her hair and sing very sweetly. And when she had done singing, he said 'Give me the comb and mirror and I'll put them back in the pouch for you.'

She handed him the comb and mirror and he put them in the pouch. He let the pouch lie for a moment in his palm: then he gave a start and said, 'What's this? The pouch is magic! I can feel the strength of it running through my fingers!'

'Nay,' said she, 'the magic is in my belt, not in the pouch.'

But he made as if he didn't believe her, so she took off her belt and put it into his hands, to let him feel for himself.

He gave a great shout then. 'Ah ha! my lady, I've got you now!' And he stuffed belt, pouch, comb, mirror and all into his pocket, laid on his oars with a will, and pulled for shore.

Did she cry? Didn't she! She wept and begged and prayed him to give her back her belt. But he wouldn't listen. He beached the boat, took her in his arms, and carried her up to his farm. And there he dumped her down and said, 'From now on, I'm master. There'll be no more nonsense with you! You'll do as you're told and behave yourself! You slapped me once, but now it's my turn!'

And he gave her a slap on her white shoulder, not to hurt her but just to prove he could do what he pleased with her.

By day he put her out with the cows on the croft. And by night he made her a bed on some straw in a corner of the cow house, and there she had to sleep. The straw got in her hair, and she begged for her comb and her mirror, but he wouldn't let her have them. He had hidden them away, together with the pouch and the belt, behind the clock on the kitchen mantelshelf.

The poor little thing got untidier and untidier: her hair was all tangled up, and she looked such a sight, flopping about on her tail with bits of straw dangling from her, that the farm-hands laughed and called after her. The dogs didn't like her, either: they snapped and snarled whenever she was near them, so she had a very bad time of it, did this little mermaid. And the worst of it was that she could look out on the water, all bright and sparkling in the sun, and couldn't get near it.

The farmer went fishing in the evenings as usual; but he locked her up in the cow house before he went; and since the other mermaids and the mermen thought she had gone home with him of her own free will, they didn't trouble him. He had calm seas and good catches all through the summer, and was well pleased with the way he had managed things. Only he was a little worried about where he had hidden the mermaid's belt and things, because she was always poking here and there looking for them, and he thought she might manage to scramble on to a chair and look behind the clock on the mantelshelf.

So it came autumn, and the corn was cut and carried. And when it was being stacked, the farmer thought what a good place the middle of a corn stack would be to hide the belt in. So, one evening, when the farm men had gone home, and the little mermaid was locked in the cow house, he took belt, pouch, mirror and comb from behind the clock, and went softly out into the stack yard, made a hole in one of the stacks, and stuffed belt and all in there.

He thought no one saw him; but someone did see him, and that was a little lad who herded the geese. He was a kind little lad; he never laughed at the mermaid, however draggly and queer she looked. He used to give her half his apple, when he had one, because he knew that mermaids like apples.

So next morning this little lad was driving the geese out on to the croft, and there was the mermaid sitting and crying.

Said he, 'Why do you always cry?'

Said she, 'Because the man has hidden my belt and my pouch and my comb and my mirror. Without my belt I can't get back to the sea. Without my comb and mirror I can't do my hair—and see what a mess I'm in!'

Said he, 'I know where they're hidden.'

'Oh!' said she, 'please, please tell me!'

Said he, 'Shall I get them for you?'

Said she, 'Oh yes, yes, *yes!*'

So the little lad ran and pulled the belt and the pouch and the comb and the mirror out of the corn stack, and brought them to the mermaid. In a moment the belt was round her waist. She didn't stop to look in the mirror and tidy herself; she rose up on the tip of her tail, and *flip!* she was gone like one flying: gone from the croft and over the beach and *splash!* into the sea.

The little lad stared and stared. First he saw nothing but the shining sea; then he saw a bright eddy; then up came the mermaid. There she was sitting on the water, combing the straw out of her golden hair and singing. It was a song all about her past miseries and her present joy, and how she would never, never be so silly as to love a human being again.

When she had done singing, and got her hair all sleek and shining, she waved to the little lad, and called out 'Catch!' She tossed up her hand, and something came flying and landed on the croft at the little lad's feet. He stooped to pick it up. It was a purse of gold.

The farmer was at market. When he came home and found the mermaid gone, didn't he rage! He couldn't think how she had got her belt back, and you may be sure the little lad never told him.

That evening the farmer thought to go fishing; but the moment he ran his boat down to the water, a huge wave rose up and washed the boat back on to the shore. And the more he tried to launch his boat, the bigger the waves that came rolling in and beat the boat back again. So he couldn't go out fishing that night, or any other night, for always the same thing happened. The sea wouldn't have him, or his boat.

Folk told him he'd better keep right away from the shore; they warned him that if he didn't, the mermaid would one day send the sea in after him and drown him. But the little mermaid never did. She remembered how she had once loved him; and perhaps her heart was a little tender towards him yet. Because, after all, he was so very handsome.

Only one thing she was quite determined about: he should stay on land where he belonged, and she would stay in the water where *she* belonged. And there should be no more meeting for them one with the other.

12

The Groach of the Isle of Lok

There was once an orphan lad called Hourn, and he fell in love with an orphan girl called Bellah. They wanted to get married and live in a little house of their own, and keep a cow and a pig and some hens and chickens. But they had no money.

So Bellah said, 'Let us both go and take service on a farm, and put by what we earn.'

And they took service on a farm. But the money they were able to put by wasn't enough to buy a hen, let alone a cow and a pig and a little house.

Said Hourn, 'Bellah, I must leave you and seek my fortune.'

'Oh no, Hourn, oh no!' said Bellah, and she began to cry.

But Hourn said, 'When bees lack honey—what do they do? They

fly till they find it. Am I to have less sense than a bee?'

So then Bellah dried her eyes, and said, 'Well, go then, if go you must. But first I have something to give you.'

She went to her room and brought down a little chest. She opened the chest and took out a bell, a knife and a little stick made of apple wood. Said she, 'Before my mother died, she gave me these three things, and they are magic. The bell will ring of itself when the one who carries it is in danger, and then it can be heard both near and far. The knife frees all things that its blade touches from any spells that have been laid upon them; and as for this dear little stick, it will carry those who get astride of it anywhere they wish to go. Take the knife, that it may guard you against evil enchantments. Take the bell, so that if you are in danger it may ring and tell me. The stick I will keep myself, so that if you are in peril I may come to you.'

So Hourn took the knife and the bell, and walked off into the wide world.

He walked a long way, but he didn't pick up any fortune on the road. And then he came to a little town by the sea. And in that town he met an old man driving a mule.

Said the old man, 'Good morning to you, friend! And whither are you bound?'

Said Hourn, 'Good morning to *you*, friend. I go to seek my fortune, that I may marry my sweetheart, and buy us a little house and a cow and a pig and some hens and chickens.'

Said the old man, 'You are bound for the Isle of Lok, then, to visit the Groach?'

Said Hourn, 'Nay, I know not. Who is the Groach?'

Said the old man, 'She is the mermaid who lives under that island over there. She owns all the treasure that ever was sunk in the sea. Many's the bold handsome youth has gone to the island seeking his fortune. But of all who have gone, none has returned.'

Said Hourn, 'I will both go and return.'

So he went down to the sea, and offered his last penny to a boatman to row him over to the Isle of Lok.

The boatman rowed him over, and left him there, and made haste back again, for the place had an ill name.

So there was Hourn, alone on the island.

On the island was a big lake, with an opening to the sea. Hourn walked along the side of the lake, and under a bush of broom he saw a little boat, shaped like a sleeping swan, with its head under its wing.

Said Hourn to himself, 'This is the queerest boat that ever I saw!'

And he took a step into the boat to look at it more closely.

No sooner was he aboard than the swan woke up, and began swimming away into the middle of the lake.

'Whoa-hey! Whoa-hee!' shouted Hourn. But the swan only swam the faster. So Hourn made to jump overboard that he might swim back to land. And before he had got one leg over the gunwale, the swan made a dive and plunged with him down to the bottom of the lake.

As soon as it touched bottom, the swan vanished, and Hourn found himself standing before the gates of a fine palace, whose golden walls shone so brightly that they made his eyes water.

The palace gates stood open, so Hourn went in, and came to a crystal hall. In the hall was a silver sofa, and on the sofa lay a maiden. And that maiden was so beautiful that Hourn lost his wits, and could only stand and stare.

'Welcome!' said the maiden. 'Handsome youths are always welcome here!' And she got up from the sofa and came to meet Hourn with outstretched arms. 'I am the Groach of the Isle of Lok,' said she. 'Who are you, and what do you seek?'

'I am Hourn,' said he. 'And I seek my fortune, that I may marry my sweetheart, and buy us a little house, and a cow and a pig, and some hens and chickens.'

'Such things are easily come by,' said the Groach. 'But now you are here, you must enjoy yourself.'

And she led him to a table on which stood a crystal cup filled with a sparkling liquid.

'We will drink to your fortune,' said she, smiling into his eyes. 'And may it be a good one!'

Then she offered Hourn the cup, but first she drank of it herself.

Hourn put the cup to his lips. He drained that cup dry. Never had he tasted anything so delicious!

But the drink was magic. It made Hourn forget about the little house and the cow and the pig and the hens and chickens. And, worse than all, it made him forget about Bellah.

'You feel better for the drink, Hourn?' said the Groach.

'Yes, I feel better,' said Hourn.

'And bolder and stronger?' said the Groach.

'And bolder and stronger,' said Hourn.

'Then it is I who will give you your heart's desire,' said the Groach. 'The wealth of the whole world is nothing to my wealth. Through the ocean there flows a magic current that brings to my palace all the treasures that ever were sunk in the sea. Would you like to share my treasures, Hourn?'

'I would indeed,' said Hourn.

The Groach flung her beautiful arms round him. 'Will you marry me and stay with me always, Hourn?'

'Yes, I will marry you, and stay with you always,' said Hourn.

The Groach laughed most merrily. 'Tomorrow shall be our wedding day,' said she. 'And now we will go fishing for our supper.'

She took down a steel fishing net from a crook on the wall, and led Hourn into a garden. At the bottom of the garden was a fish pond. The Groach dipped her net into the pond and sang out: 'Come, miller; come, lawyer; come, tailor; come, princeling!' And at each call a rainbow-coloured fish put its head up out of the pond and jumped into the net.

Carrying the four fishes in the net, the Groach bade Hourn follow her back into the palace, and into a big kitchen. And there she threw the fish into a golden pot over the fire.

'They will soon be ready to eat,' she said, 'for the water boils and bubbles.'

But above the bubbling of the water, Hourn seemed to hear the bubbling of little voices.

'What is that whispering in the pot?' he asked.

'It is only the wood crackling on the fire,' said the Groach.

But it didn't sound like the crackling of wood to Hourn.

'There it is again!' he said.

'The water boils and the fishes jump,' said the Groach.

But the noises grew louder and louder. And they sounded to Hourn like the cries of men.

'What *is* it I hear? What *is* it?' he cried.

'It is only the crickets singing on the hearth,' said the Groach. 'But now *I* will sing to you—my voice is prettier than theirs.'

She began to sing, and her song was magic. It made Hourn deaf to the noises in the pot.

When the fishes were cooked, the Groach took them out of the pot, laid them in a golden dish, carried the dish into the crystal room and set it on the table.

'Sit down and eat, my Hourn,' she said. 'You must be hungry. I will go to the cellar for wine, and join you again.'

Hourn sat down at the table, and took the knife that Bellah had given him out of his pocket. But no sooner had the knife touched the fishes, than the fishes vanished. And there by the table stood four handsome young men.

'Hourn, Hourn, save yourself!' they whispered.

'Then—it was you who cried to me out of the pot?'

'Yes, yes, it was we who cried out. Like you we came to the Isle of Lok seeking our fortunes. Like you we drank from the cup of the Groach. Like you we each in turn agreed to marry her. And no sooner was the ceremony over than she turned us into fishes, as she had turned to fishes all those who came before us. They are in the pond now—where you, Hourn, will presently join them.'

Hourn gave a leap into the air, as if he already felt himself frizzling in the pot. Then he made a rush to the door, thinking to escape. But the Groach met him on the threshold. She threw the steel net over his head. Then there was no Hourn any more; there was only a little green frog peeping sadly through the meshes of the net.

'You shall go and play with the others,' laughed the Groach.

And she carried him off and dropped him into the fish pond.

Then the little green frog remembered Bellah again, and wept.

Bellah was churning butter in the farm dairy when she heard the loud tinkling of a bell. Dropping the handle of the churn, she ran for her stick, and hurried away with it out of the farm to the crossroads. There she leaned the stick upright against a mile stone, and sang out:

> '*Little staff of apple tree,*
> *Over the earth, or over the sea,*
> *To where my love is, carry me!*'

And immediately the stick turned into a little white horse. Bellah got up on his back, and away he galloped.

'Faster, faster, my littie horse!' cried Bellah. 'The wind is swifter than the swallow, the lightning is swifter than the wind, but you, my little horse, must be swifter than all three.'

Then, indeed, the earth whizzed away under that little horse's hoofs as if he were a leaf whirled along in a tempest, until they came to a black cliff, rising sheer into the clouds; and there the little horse pulled up and turned into a stick again, for no horse that ever lived could scale that cliff. And there was no way round it.

So Bellah sang again:

> '*Little staff of apple tree,*
> *Up in the air now carry me,*
> *That I may set my true love free.*'

Then the stick turned into a great bird. Bellah perched herself between the bird's wings. And the bird flew with her to the top of the cliff.

On the top of the cliff was a nest made of clay and lined with moss; and in the nest was a tiny man, sitting on six stone eggs. The tiny man was burned nearly black with the sun, and the hair on his head was flaming red.

When he saw Bellah, this tiny man clapped his hands and cried in a shrill voice, 'At last you have come to set me free!'

'I will gladly set you free, if I can,' said Bellah. 'But who are you?'

'I am the unhappy husband of the Groach of the Isle of Lok,' said the tiny man. '*She* put me here. And here I must sit till these stone eggs hatch out,'

'But that will be never, my poor little man! So how can I set you free?'

'It needn't be never,' said the tiny man. 'The eggs will hatch out quickly enough if you can outwit the Groach. And then, too, you will be able to deliver Hourn, who is in her power.'

'Oh, tell me how to do that!' cried Bellah. 'And if I have to go round the whole world on my bended knees, I will do it!'

'It shouldn't be as difficult as all that,' said the tiny man. 'You must dress yourself as a young man, and then seek out the Groach. She has a steel net that she catches people in. So when you find her, be quick and clever. Get hold of that net, throw it over her and call out, "Take your true shape." Then she will turn into a purple-spotted serpent. But don't be afraid—the serpent will never get out of that net. In the garden near the fish pond, you will find a deep, deep hole with a great stone beside it. Fling net and serpent into the hole and roll the stone down on top of them. That's all.'

'But Hourn, Hourn!' cried Bellah. 'You haven't told me how to rescue Hourn!'

'I can't tell you everything,' said the tiny man, rather crossly. 'You must use your wits—and the magic knife.'

'But where am I to find a young man's clothes?'

'Ah, that I *can* tell you,' said the tiny man. He pulled four red hairs out of his head, and blew on them. Immediately the four hairs turned into four little tailors. The first tailor carried a cabbage, the second a pair of scissors, the third a needle, the fourth a reel of thread. And the four little tailors seated themselves cross-legged in the nest, and began making a suit of clothes for Bellah.

With one of the leaves of the cabbage, they made her a coat; with another leaf they made her a waistcoat, and with two more leaves a pair of wide breeches. They made her a hat from the white heart of the cabbage, and a pair of shoes from the thick stalk. And when Bellah had put on all these things, there she was, as handsome a young man as you would wish to see, dressed in green velvet, with a white felt hat, and shoes of the softest white leather.

Then the four little tailors turned back into four red hairs and drifted away into the clouds; the stick that was lying on the cliff top turned back into a bird. Bellah perched herself between the bird's wings, waved goodbye to the tiny man, and was carried by the bird to the Isle of Lok.

And there, by the side of the lake, under the bush of broom, was the swan boat. So Bellah bade the bird change back into a stick, and with the stick in her hand, she got into the boat and was carried down to the Groach's palace.

The Groach was lying on her silver sofa. When she saw Bellah, she rose up and came to meet her, holding out her hands. 'Welcome!' she said. 'Handsome young men are always welcome here, and you are the handsomest young man that ever I set eyes on!'

And she led Bellah to the table, where the magic liquid sparkled in the crystal cup.

There was something else on the table; and that was the magic knife that Hourn had left there. Bellah's heart gave a jump when she saw it.

'Oh, what a pretty little knife!' she said.

And she picked it up.

'A mere trifle,' said the Groach, 'left there by one of my stupid servants. It is not worth anything.'

'Then may I keep it?' said Bellah.

'You may keep it, if you fancy it,' said the Groach. 'But come, let us drink of the loving cup!'

So the Groach put the magic cup to her own lips, and then handed it to Bellah. But Bellah touched the cup with the knife, and the magic died out of it. She drained the cup dry, but she didn't forget Hourn, nor yet the little house and the cow and the pig and the hens and chickens. For what she drank was pure water.

'And now,' said the Groach, 'we will go and fish for our supper.' She took the steel net from its crook on the wall; and Bellah put the magic knife in her pocket and followed the Groach down to the fish pond. The pond was all in commotion: the fishes were swimming about wildly, and leaping from the water after flies. And their rainbow colours glittered in the bright sunshine.

'Oh what beautiful, beautiful creatures!' cried Bellah. 'I should never weary of watching them!'

'Would you like to stay here always, and share my treasures?' said the Groach. 'I can make you rich.'

'I should like well enough to be rich,' said Bellah.

'Then you have only to marry me,' said the Groach. 'Oh, don't say no, for you are surely the most beautiful youth in all the world, and I love you dearly.'

'Well, I won't say no,' laughed Bellah. 'But if you love me as you say, lend me your net. I have a fancy to go fishing myself.'

'It is not easy to catch my fishes,' said the Groach. 'But take the net, and try your luck.'

Bellah took the net and stooped over the pool. Then she turned swiftly and flung the net over the Groach's head.

'Take your true shape, wicked one!' she cried.

And the Groach vanished; and in the net there writhed and hissed a purple-spotted snake.

The snake struggled hard to tear the net asunder, but the steel mesh held firm. Bellah ran with the net to the deep hole in the ground, flung both net and snake into the hole, and rolled down the stone on top of them. Then she went back to the pond.

And what should she see but a great procession of fishes rising out of the pond and coming to meet her.

'This is our lord and master,' they cried hoarsely, 'who has saved us from the net of steel and the cauldron of gold!'

'And who will now restore you to your proper shapes,' said Bellah.

She took the magic knife from her pocket, and was just about to touch the foremost of the fishes with it, when she caught sight of a little green frog. The frog went down on his knees before her; his little paws were crossed over his little heart, round his neck hung a little bell, and his eyes were streaming with tears.

'Hourn!' cried Bellah. 'Oh, my Hourn, is this you?'

'Yes, I am Hourn,' croaked the little green frog.

So Bellah touched him with the magic knife, and there he was in his own proper shape again; and springing up, he took her in his arms.

That was a happy moment for them both, you may be sure!

'But we mustn't forget the others,' said Bellah.

So she began touching each fish in turn with the knife, and as she touched them, each in turn sprang up a handsome young man. There were so many of them that it took a long time; and she had but just restored the last fish to its proper shape when there came a buzzing overhead, and looking up they saw the tiny man with the red hair riding through the air in a little carriage drawn by six cockchafers.

The cockchafers brought the carriage to the ground, and the tiny man leaped out.

'The eggs have hatched!' cried he. 'You have broken the spell that bound me. Come and get your reward!'

He led them down into a cave under the palace, and the cave was filled with gold and jewels.

'Come, load up! Load up!' he shouted. 'Here is a pile of sacks. You may fill them all. Get busy! Load up! Load up!'

So Bellah and Hourn and all the handsome young men got busy filling the sacks with the gold and jewels, whilst the tiny man watched them and laughed. And when the sacks were full, Bellah leant her stick against the cave wall, and sang out:

'Little staff of apple tree,
Carry us all where we wish to be.'

Then the stick turned itself into a winged chariot, large enough to hold them every one, and the treasure sacks as well. So they all got in, and waved goodbye to the tiny man, who was still laughing. And the chariot flew with them up through the lake and away back home.

Bellah and Hourn were married that very day. But there was no need for them now to be content with a little house and one cow and one pig and a few hens and chickens. With the treasure from the sacks they were able to buy themselves a big estate, and give to each of the handsome young men a farm for himself.

And they all prospered and lived happily to the end of their days.

13

The Geese and the Golden Chain

O nce upon a time there was a girl called Marziella, who lived with her brother, Pedro, in a little house by the sea. Pedro was a sailor; and when he was off on his voyages, Marziella was quite alone. Then sometimes she would go in and chat with her neighbours—a widow woman and her daughter, Puccia.

Well, one day news came that Pedro's ship would soon be home. So Marziella baked some little cakes, and the cakes smelled good.

'I will eat just one,' she said to herself. Then she remembered that she must go to the fountain for water. So, with the water pitcher on her head, and the little cake in her hand, off she went to the fountain.

She filled her pitcher, set it down, and was just going to eat the little cake when an old woman came hobbling along.

'My little pretty one,' said the old woman, 'my stomach is quite empty. Give me a bit of your cake, and may heaven send you good fortune!'

'If your stomach is empty, mother,' said Marziella, 'it's not a bit of the cake you shall have, but the whole of it. And I wish it were three times as big!'

The old woman took the cake. She was a long time eating it, because, with every bite she took, the cake grew bigger. She made a meal of it—enough to fill anyone's stomach. It was only when she was full that there was no cake left.

Marziella watched her, and said, 'I think you must be a fairy, mother?'

'May be,' said the old woman. 'But fairy or no, my little pretty one, I have nothing to give you but a comb. Will you take that with my blessing?'

'I will gladly take it,' said Marziella, 'if you can spare it.'

'Pooh!' said the old woman. 'Anyone can spare a little comb! But two promises go with it.'

'And what are the promises, mother?'

'The first is that you will never use any comb but this to comb your hair. And the second that you will let no one else use it.'

Marziella made the two promises and took the comb, which was a very ordinary-looking one. Then she said goodbye to the old woman and went home again, carrying the full water-pitcher on her head, and the comb in her hand. She set the pitcher down on the doorstep, and as she did so a great wind came roaring round the house and blew her long hair into her eyes. So she ran indoors, stood before a looking glass, and combed back her hair with the comb the old woman had given her.

Oh! Oh! Oh! Showers of pearls were falling out of her hair and rolling about the floor! She picked up a handful of them and ran in to her neighbours. 'Look! Look!' And she told them about the old woman and the comb.

'Lend *me* the comb!' cried Puccia.

But Marziella said she couldn't do that. She had promised the old woman she would lend it to no one.

'Then comb again, and let us see!' said the widow.

Yes, Marziella would do that. She combed and combed. The pearls fell out in showers. The widow wouldn't let her stop combing till the kitchen floor was thick with them. Then the widow and Puccia gathered them all up in their aprons.

'We can keep them of course?' said the widow.

'Of course!' said Marziella.

So the widow put the pearls in a big box, and Marziella went back into her own little house.

'Ah ha! my girl,' said the widow to Puccia. 'We are going to be rich for the rest of our lives!'

But when she went to look again into the box where she had put the pearls, there was nothing in the box but a few withered leaves. She stamped with rage then. She said the old woman was a witch, and Marziella was a witch; but she would get even with them yet!

When her brother Pedro came home, Marziella showed him the comb and the pearls, and said, 'What shall we do with them?'

'You must string them up into bunches,' said Pedro. 'And on my next voyage I will take them to the king of the country I am going to. He is somewhat hot-tempered, but he is just. He will give us a fair price,'

So Marziella strung all the pearls that fell from her hair into large bunches, and Pedro took the bunches with him on his next voyage and showed them to the king of the country.

The king said, 'I have never seen such magnificent pearls! Where did you get them?'

Pedro told him, and the king said, 'Go home and fetch your sister. If what you say is true, I will make her my queen. But if you are lying to me, I will have your head!'

So Pedro sailed off home to fetch Marziella.

When the widow next door heard that Marziella was going to be a queen, she turned yellow with envy.

'Why should a silly little thing like Marziella live in a palace and wear a crown,' said the widow to Puccia, 'and you, who are worth a dozen of her, have to live in a cottage and wear nothing better than a straw bonnet?' Why indeed? Puccia felt that way too.

But they put smiles on their faces and pretended to be delighted with Marziella's good fortune. And the widow said, 'We have always been good neighbours. Now that you are going to be so rich and noble, will you do us a neighbourly turn?'

'I will gladly,' said Marziella. 'What is it?'

'Oh, just to take us along with you,' said the widow. 'And when you are queen ask the king to give us some humble position at court.'

'You may be sure I will do what I can,' said Marziella.

So they all embarked, Marziella and Pedro and the widow and

Puccia. And when they had been many days and nights at sea, the weather became sultry.

So one evening the widow said, 'We are all hot and thirsty. I have made a cooling drink. Come, we will all drink of it and refresh ourselves.' She took four glasses and poured out the drink. But into Marziella's glass and into Pedro's glass, she put a sleeping potion.

Marziella and Pedro slept soundly that night: nothing would wake them. The widow went to where Marziella lay and took the comb from her. Then she bound Marziella's feet together and tied an iron weight to them. She bound Marziella's arms and tied another weight to them. And then she called Puccia, and together they carried Marziella to the stern of the ship and heaved her overboard.

It was deep darkness there in the stern of the ship. The sailors did not see what the widow was doing. But when it was done, she ran about the ship screaming, 'The girl's jumped overboard! The girl's jumped overboard!'

The captain put the ship about, he lowered a boat, the sailors rowed and searched. They couldn't find Marziella. She had sunk down, down, deep down. The sailors ran to Pedro and tried to wake him. They couldn't wake him; he slept soundly, soundly.

The ship sailed on. It was two days before Pedro woke, and then the ship was near to port. Pedro rubbed his eyes, yawned and said, 'Where is Marziella? We must get ready to land!'

Oh! Oh! How the widow wept, how Puccia wailed! They told Pedro the sad news. He tore his hair and cried, 'What shall I do? What shall I do? The king will kill me!'

'I have found poor Marziella's comb,' said the widow, pretending to sob. 'The king has never seen Marziella. Let us give Puccia the comb, and take her to the king in Marziella's place.'

'No, no, we can't do that!' cried Pedro.

'What else *can* we do?' said the widow. 'We must make the best of a bad business. If you are willing to lose your head, I am not.'

Pedro wasn't willing to lose his head, so he agreed. The widow dressed Puccia in her best clothes, and when they landed Pedro took her to the king. The king said, 'Oh, you are come, are you?'

He didn't like the look of Puccia. What had he been expecting? Some one more rare, more beautiful. *This* girl—well, her hair didn't look of the pearl-dropping kind. The king scowled and tugged at his beard. But he said, 'Oh, all right, girl—comb your hair!'

Puccia shook down her hair and began to comb. Oh dear! No pearls—nothing but tangles. She combed and combed; but the more she combed, the worse grew the tangles. Her head looked like a field of thistles. The king shook his fist and stamped. 'You have all deceived me!' he shouted.

'Oh no,' said the widow. 'The girl is tired. Wait until tomorrow morning; then you will have pearls in plenty.'

The king agreed to wait. 'But if in the morning there are no pearls, I will have you hanged, all three of you!'

They went to bed. Puccia stormed at her mother all night. Pedro lay awake shivering with fear. The widow took some of the pearls that Pedro had brought with him and fastened them into Puccia's hair. 'At any rate you can comb *these* out!' she said.

Could she? The pearls were in Puccia's hair all right when she

stood before the king next morning. But when she began to comb—
those pearls turned into thistles. The more she combed, the faster
fell the thistles. They lay piled about the king's feet. He stamped on
them and raged.

'Hanging is too good for you!' he bawled. 'Get out of my sight!'

He didn't really want to hang anybody: he was better than he made
himself out to be. He had the widow and Puccia whipped out of the
palace, and Pedro he put to herd the geese.

The widow and Puccia wandered on the sea shore. The widow
said, 'Comb again, Puccia, comb again!'

Puccia combed again. What happened? Down fell a shower of little
crabs. Puccia screamed and flung the comb into the sea. And then, as
the ship they had come in was setting sail again, they went aboard,
and the good-natured captain took them home.

Pedro watched the ship sail away. He shed tears. He let the geese
wander where they would, and they wandered down to the shore.
Pedro found a little hut made of straw. He went into it and sat and
wept. Nobody had ever been unhappier. To herd geese was bad enough;
dread of what the king might yet do to him was worse; and worst
of all was the thought of Marziella lying drowned at the bottom of
the sea.

But Marziella wasn't lying drowned at the bottom of the sea. For
a merman who happened to come swimming along had seen her.
He had untied the weights from her hands and feet, carried her off
to his palace, and revived her with life-giving water.

The merman looked into Marziella's eyes and said,

'Sweet! Sweet! Sweet!
Fair is the sun, and fair is the moon,
But you, maiden, are fairer still.
Live with me, and be my wife!'

But Marziella said, 'I cannot answer you until I have seen my brother.'

So the merman took her under his arm and swam till he came close to the shore of the king's country. Then he fastened a gold chain round Marziella's ankle and said, 'Now you may go up out of the water. But if you stay too long I shall pull you back. Your hair is tangled—why don't you comb it?'

Marziella said, 'I can't. I have lost my comb.'

The merman said, 'Here is one I have just picked up,'

And he gave Marziella her own comb, which Puccia had flung into the sea.

So whilst Pedro sat weeping in the hut, and the geese were waddling about on the beach, Marziella came up out of the sea. She had a basket and a bowl with her. The basket was full of little sweet cakes; the bowl was full of rosewater. She fed the geese with the sweet cakes, and gave them the rosewater to drink. The geese became as big as sheep, and so fat that they could hardly open their eyes.

When the geese were fed, Marziella sat on a rock and combed her hair; showers of pearls fell out of it. She was looking round everywhere for Pedro. She couldn't see him: he lay in the straw hut and wept.

At sunset the merman gave a jerk to the golden chain round Marziella's ankle. She went down again under the sea. The fat geese went waddling home, and Pedro came out of the hut and followed them. The geese pushed their way into a little garden under the king's window, and there they stretched out their necks and sang:

'*Pirie! Pirie! Pirie!*
Fair is the sun, fair is the moon,
But the maid who feeds us is fairer still!'

The king looked out of the window. My goodness—what enormous geese! He sent for Pedro. Pedro came shivering. Was the king now going to torture him?

But the king said, 'What food have you been giving my geese?'

Pedro said, 'Nothing but the grass of the fields.'

The king said, 'You lie! Get out of my sight!'

And Pedro was glad enough to go.

Next morning he again let the geese wander where they would. Again the geese went down to the shore; and Pedro sat in the hut and wept. And again Marziella came up out of the sea with a basket full of sweet cakes and a bowl of rosewater. The geese ate and drank; they grew and grew; they were as big as calves. Marziella sat on a rock; she combed her hair, showers of pearls fell out of it. She looked round everywhere for Pedro. She could not see him: he was lying on the floor of the hut, weeping.

At sunset the merman jerked the golden chain. Marziella went down under the water; the huge geese waddled home, and Pedro came out of the hut and followed them. The geese pushed their way into the little garden under the king's window; they stretched out their necks and sang:

> '*Pirie! Pirie! Pirie!*
> *Fair is the sun, fair is the moon,*
> *But the maid who feeds us is fairer still!*'

They did this every day, and every day they grew bigger and bigger. They grew as big as horses. But Pedro said he had given them nothing but the grass of the fields.

So the king sent a trusty servant to follow Pedro and see where he took the geese.

The servant watched. In the evening he went back to the king.

'My king, I have seen a wonder!'

'What wonder?'

'I saw Pedro go into a little hut made of straw. I pulled out some wisps of straw and made a hole. I peeped through the hole and saw Pedro lying on the floor, weeping.'

'There is nothing wonderful in that!' said the king.

'I saw the geese go down to the edge of the water—'

'And there is nothing wonderful in *that!*' said the king.

'I saw a maiden rise up out of the water—'

'*Out of the water!*" said the king. 'If you are not lying, this is indeed a wonder!'

'The maiden was carrying a basket of sweet cakes and a bowl of rosewater. The geese ate and drank. But oh, my king,

'Fair is the sun, fair is the moon,
But the maiden who fed the geese is fairer still!'

The king said, 'I know all that! The geese have told it to me often enough! But when the geese had finished eating, and grown, I suppose, as big as elephants—what happened next?'

'The maiden sat on a rock. She combed her hair, and showers of pearls fell out of it,'

'*Showers of pearls*, did you say?' shouted the king. And he ran out of the palace and made for the shore.

But it was evening: Marziella had gone down under the water again. All the king saw was the flock of geese, as big as horses, waddling home, and Pedro drearily following them.

The geese gathered round the king, stretched out their necks, and began to sing,

'Pirie! Pirie! Pirie!
Fair is the sun—'

'Be quiet, can't you?' shouted the king. 'I wish to speak to Pedro!' And the king told Pedro what the servant had seen.

'Yes, yes, it is Marziella!' cried Pedro. 'It must surely be Marziella!' There was no more weeping for him after that!

Next morning Pedro didn't go to the hut: he followed the geese down to the shore with a merry heart, and the king went with him.

And when Marziella came up out of the sea, Pedro rushed to take her in his arms.

'My sister! My sister!' cried Pedro.

'My brother! My brother!' cried Marziella.

'My queen! My queen!' cried the king.

Marziella scattered the cakes from her basket, and set down the bowl of rosewater. Then she sat on a rock and combed her hair. The pearls fell round her in showers; and she told the king and Pedro all her story.

The king said, 'Pedro, my lad, I have wronged you. But I will make amends. When Marziella is my queen, I will give you a dukedom. Come, let us all three go back to the palace!'

But Marziella said, 'Don't you see this golden chain fastened to my ankle? I am the merman's prisoner. When the sun sets he drags me down again under the sea: and tomorrow when the sun sets, he will marry me.'

'I will run my sword through his scaly body!' cried the king.

'You shall do no such thing!' said Marziella. 'He saved my life. And he has been good to me, in his way.'

'But you cannot love him!' cried the king. 'If you tell me you love him, I shall drown myself!'

Marziella laughed. 'No need for that, my king. Come tomorrow morning with a file: file through the chain and slip me out of it.'

'Then you don't love him?' cried the king.

Marziella laughed again. 'One need not love, and yet one may be grateful,' she said.

That is nearly the end of the story. Next morning the king went down to the shore with a file. Marziella came up out of the water; the king quickly filed through the golden chain and set her free. Under the sea the merman felt the chain go slack. He put his head up over a wave, and saw Marziella and the king running up the beach.

'Marziella! Marziella!' wailed the merman.

It was sadness for him, but it was gladness for everyone else. The king and Marziella had a splendid wedding. Pedro got his dukedom. Marziella combed her hair and gave away pearls in handfuls to anyone who asked for them. She went on doing this. The people called her their Queen of Pearls. They sent out ships laden with pearls to every port in the world. And soon there was not a single poor person in all that happy country.

14

Merman Rosmer

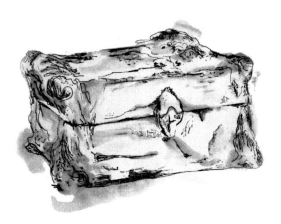

There was once a proud woman called Lady Hillers, who had three sons and one daughter; and she had a mind to build herself a splendid castle on a cliff above the sea.

People said to her, 'Don't build there!'

Lady Hillers said, 'And pray, why not?'

The people said, 'Because of Merman Rosmer.'

Lady Hillers said, 'Does Merman Rosmer own the earth as well as the ocean, that I may not build where I please?'

And the people said, 'Merman Rosmer has long, long arms. Your daughter, Svanie, is very, very pretty: and Merman Rosmer has a fancy for pretty things.'

And Lady Hillers said, 'Bah! I can well take care of my own daughter!'

So she built her castle, and a grand castle it was.

But she was wrong, and the people were right. One morning, when Svanie was leaning on the castle wall, looking down at the sea, Merman Rosmer looked up and saw her. He reached up his long, long arms and carried her away.

Lady Hillers wrung her hands and wept. And the people said, 'There, what did we tell her? But oh no! She wouldn't listen!'

So then Lady Hillers' eldest son said, 'Mother, give me a ship. I will sail away and seek my sister, and I will not come back without her.'

So Lady Hillers built him a magnificent ship, and off he sailed.

But he didn't find Svanie, and he had to come back without her, because Merman Rosmer met him on his way. And Merman Rosmer gave the sea one blow with his fist, and the ship another blow. He set the whole ocean boiling, and beat the ship back the way it had come. He drove it on to the rocks under the castle, and wrecked it there. And Lady Hillers' eldest son and his sailors crawled up the cliff more dead than alive.

Then the second son went to Lady Hillers and said, 'Mother, give *me* a ship! I will sail away to seek my sister. Perhaps I shall be more fortunate.'

So Lady Hillers built him a fine great ship, and off he sailed. But he wasn't more fortunate. Merman Rosmer met him on his way, gave the ocean one blow, and the ship another blow, and drove him back and wrecked him, just as he had wrecked his brother.

Then the youngest son, whose name was Peterkin, said, 'Mother, give me a ship. I, too, wish to sail away and seek my sister.'

But Lady Hillers wouldn't give him a ship, because he was only a little lad.

'What do you know about ships?' she said. 'If Merman Rosmer raises a storm, you will never weather it. Your brothers were wrecked, it is true, but at least they came home. If Merman Rosmer raises a storm against you, you will not come home.'

But Peterkin was a clever little fellow, and he said to himself, 'Yes, if Merman Rosmer recognizes me he will raise a storm. But why should he recognize me?'

So he disguised himself as a fisher lad, and went into the town, and bought a little rowing boat, and rowed away. And when Merman Rosmer saw that little fisher lad rowing in his little boat, he thought no harm at all. He made the sea calm for him, and let him row on.

Peterkin rowed and rowed, and came at last to an island, and there he landed. In that island there was a cave, and in the cave there was a passage, going down and down and farther down till it came to the grand golden palace belonging to Merman Rosmer.

So Peterkin went down that passage, and came to the palace, and hid behind a pillar in the courtyard till he saw Merman Rosmer come out. And then in he ran, and found Svanie in the kitchen, cooking the merman's supper.

When Svanie saw Peterkin she threw up her arms and cried out, 'Oh Peterkin, Peterkin, why have you come! If Merman Rosmer sees you, he will break your neck with one flip of his finger!'

'I have come to set you free and take you home,' said Peterkin.

But Svanie hustled him away into a corner behind the wood pile, and there she bade him stay, and not for his life to stir, or sneeze, or cough, or make a sound.

By and by Merman Rosmer came in again.

And Svanie said, 'Now here is your supper ready. Come, eat and drink!'

So Merman Rosmer sat him down and ate and drank. And when he was full and feeling pleased, he held Svanie in his long arms, and she stroked his great hand and said, 'There is a little fisher lad come from home to visit me. Only a little lad, dear Rosmer—you won't harm him, will you?'

'No, I won't harm him,' said Merman Rosmer. 'Where is he? Let me see him!'

So Svanie bade Peterkin come out from behind the wood pile, and Merman Rosmer said, 'So! I know you, my little lad! I watched you rowing in your little boat, and I made the sea calm for you.'

And he picked up Peterkin, and gave him a flip or two with his great fingers.

Peterkin was black and blue all over from the hard strength of those fingers, and Svanie said, 'Sir Rosmer, will you never learn the power that is in your ten fingers, but you must go flipping a poor little lad?'

'Well, well,' said Merman Rosmer, 'rub some ointment on him, and put him to bed.'

Peterkin stayed in Merman Rosmer's palace for quite a long time. He served Merman Rosmer in every way he could, and Merman Rosmer came to like him.

But Svanie and Peterkin were always plotting together on ways to escape. So one day Svanie sat herself on Merman Rosmer's lap and said, 'I had a dream last night. And in my dream I saw our little fisher lad's mother mourning for her son and shedding bitter tears. Dear Merman Rosmer, do you think we should send him home?'

'Well, well, I'll take him home,' said Merman Rosmer.

'And if we could send a little present with him,' said Svanie, 'I think it would cheer his mother's heart.'

'Well, well, I'll carry a present with him,' said Merman Rosmer. 'What shall it be?'

'Just some little trifle,' said Svanie. 'For I think you are not rich, Sir Rosmer?'

'Not rich!' shouted Merman Rosmer. 'Who says I'm not rich? There is no one in the sea or on the land who possesses a quarter of the riches I possess!'

'Well then, perhaps a little bag of copper money,' said the artful Svanie. 'If you're sure you can spare it?'

'Copper money be blowed!' shouted Merman Rosmer. 'Is that what you call a gift?'

'Then perhaps a little chest of silver money,' said Svanie. 'Just a very little one.'

'Why a little one?' shouted Merman Rosmer. 'And why *silver* money? Come with me, girl, and I'll show you!'

He took Svanie to his treasure chamber that was piled up with gold. He dragged in a huge chest and filled it with the gold. 'There,' said he, 'that's the way *I* do things! No one shall call *me* poor or stingy! This is the present our little fisher lad shall take home to his mother to dry her tears! And tomorrow morning we will start on our journey, he and I.'

'It's a long, long way,' said Svanie. 'You will have to start very early.'

'I *shall* start very early!' said Merman Rosmer.

'Then I will say goodbye to our little fisher lad tonight,' said Svanie. 'For I don't like getting up early.'

She went to Peterkin and kissed him and said, 'Goodbye, little fisher lad. Give my love to your mother when you get home.'

But when they were all in bed, and the palace shook with Merman Rosmer's snores, what did Svanie do? She got up softly, very softly, crept downstairs quietly, quietly, and away with her into the treasure chamber. She emptied the gold out of the chest, she stacked the gold neatly away, and then she got into the chest herself, and drew down the lid.

In the morning, Merman Rosmer rose early. He took Peterkin on his back, and the chest under his arm, and swam and swam till he came to the cliff where Lady Hillers' castle stood. He stretched out a long, long arm, heaved the chest on to the top of the cliff, and set Peterkin up to stand beside it.

'Off with you into the town now, my little fisher lad,' he said. 'And fetch a horse and cart to carry the chest full of gold home to your mother. Now I am going back to my Svanie.'

Peterkin waited till Merman Rosmer had dived down under the sea, and then he ran into the castle and called men out to carry in the chest.

'Mother,' said he to Lady Hillers, 'I have brought you a wonderful present!'

But Lady Hillers said, 'What is the use of your bringing me presents, if you can't bring me Svanie?'

'Well, open the chest.'

Lady Hillers opened the chest.

'Oh! Oh! Oh!'

Out jumped Svanie.

So they rejoiced all of them together. But in the midst of their rejoicing they heard a roar from the sea. They ran to the windows and saw the waves leaping up to heaven, and the foam flying to mingle with the clouds. For Merman Rosmer, having been home and found Svanie gone, was coming back in a most terrible rage.

'I'll teach you to play tricks on me!' he roared: and the waves roared with him and the cliffs echoed.

But nobody stopped to wait for his coming: Lady Hillers, and her three sons, and Svanie and the servants ran out of the castle and fled inland. And well they did, for Merman Rosmer reached up his long, long arms, and doubled up his two great fists, and struck the castle such a blow that it tumbled down. Then he went back to his palace under the sea and sulked.

He sulked for a long time. And then one day he looked out and saw a mermaid swimming by. The mermaid was very, very pretty, and Merman Rosmer had a fancy for pretty things. So he reached out his long, long arms, and lifted the mermaid into his palace. The mermaid was proud to be the wife of such a great strong fellow; and so Merman Rosmer was happy again.

As for Lady Hillers, she built herself another castle far inland; but not nearly such a grand one. And the people said, 'Pride goes before a fall. If she'd listened to us in the beginning, she'd have saved herself a lot of trouble.'

15

The Lake Maiden

A young shepherd lived with his widowed mother. One hot day he
drove his flock to feed on the grass by the borders of a lake. The
sheep strayed here and there, nibbling the grass, and the shepherd
sat down on the edge of the lake to eat his dinner of barley-bread
and cheese.

He looked idly at the water, and thought how pretty it was, smooth
and bright, reflecting the blue sky and the white clouds. He looked
down at his bread and cheese. Then he looked again at the water
and sprang to his feet in astonishment. He might well be astonished;
for there, seated on the water, combing her long hair, and using the
lake as her looking glass, was the most beautiful maiden he had ever
set eyes on.

The shepherd stood staring as if he had lost his wits. He was holding out his bread and cheese to the maiden, but he scarcely knew what he was doing. As to the maiden, she was looking at him and smiling; and lightly, lightly, she was gliding over the water towards him.

So there was the shepherd staring, and the maiden coming closer and closer. She was so close now that he could touch her, and he put the bread into her hand. She took one bite of it, laughed, and gave it back to him, singing out:

> '*Hard-baked is thy bread,*
> *It is not easy to catch me!*'

And then she went back into the lake and disappeared.

If ever there was a lad who fell in love at first sight, our shepherd was that lad. He left his dinner untouched, and all day he stood like one in a dream, thinking of the maiden. When in the evening he went home to his mother, he was babbling like a lunatic. 'Mother, I'm in love! Mother, I'm in love!'

And he told her all about the maiden.

'If I can't get her, I shall die!' he said.

His mother said, 'Seems she didn't like your well-baked bread. Perhaps it is unbaked bread she is used to. Tomorrow you shall take her some dough.'

The lad went to bed. He didn't sleep: all night he was thinking of the maiden. In the morning his mother gave him a lump of dough, and said, 'Try her with this.'

The lad drove his sheep to the lake. He looked for the maiden: there was no sight of her. He stood all day by the lake, looking, looking.

At sunset he called over the water. 'I will not leave this spot till I see you! I will stand here till I die of old age!'

Then she came. First there was only the setting sun, blazing on the water. Next, there she was, walking in the blaze of sunset over the water towards him. She was smiling; she came close; she stretched out her hand. He put the dough into it. She took one bite. She gave it back to him, and sang out:

> 'Unbaked is thy bread,
> I will not have thee.'

Then she was gone again. The shepherd burst out blubbering like a baby. He drove his sheep home and said to his mother, 'She won't have me! I shall die!'

'No, you won't die,' said his mother. 'Tomorrow you shall take some medium-baked bread.'

So next morning he got up very early, took the medium-baked bread, and drove his sheep to the lake for the third time. And this time—well, if she wasn't there waiting for him, fresh as a daisy and smiling into his eyes. He held out the medium-baked bread to her. She took it, ate it all, and sang out:

> 'Good is thy bread,
> Now I will have thee.'

The shepherd thought to take her in his arms. What a maiden! One moment she was there, smiling at him; and the next moment she was gone under the water. He thought he would go mad. He called and entreated. Not a ripple on the water! If she had left him—what use for him to live? Now he would throw himself into the lake and be done with life!

He nearly did, too. But look! Something was rising from the water, and coming closer and closer to him: a majestic old man, very tall, very handsome, with nothing on him but wreaths of water lilies; and with him *two* maidens, so exactly alike that the shepherd couldn't tell which was the one he loved and which wasn't.

'So you wish to wed my daughter,' said the majestic old man. 'But which daughter? If you can tell me that, you shall have her.'

What could the shepherd say or do? He stared and stared. The maidens were both laughing at him. Surely it was the maiden on the old man's right hand that he loved! No, surely it was the one on his left hand!

He was in despair; but help was coming. The maiden on the old man's left hand moved her foot the tiniest, tiniest step forward. That was enough! The foot had a golden sandal on it, and the strap was broken. He remembered that broken strap! He gave a leap towards her, and took her hand.

'This is the one!' he cried.

'You are right,' said the old man. 'Take her, and be a kind and faithful husband. For her dowry I will give her as many sheep, cattle, goats and horses as she can count in one breath. But if you should ever strike her with earth and with iron, back she shall come to me, and all her stock come with her.'

'Strike her!' cried the shepherd. 'That could never be!'

And the old man said, 'Well, I have warned you.'

He put the maiden that was to be the shepherd's wife to stand by the edge of the lake. 'Count for cattle!' said he.

The maiden drew a deep breath and began to count very fast: 'One, two, three, four, five, one-two-three-four-five.' She counted in fives because she could count longer that way without taking another breath; and every time she said *'five'* five cows came up out of the water. She got twenty of them, and a fine bull, too, before she had done with that breath.

Then it was 'Count for sheep,' and she managed to get twenty-five. And then it was 'Count for goats', and she got them, two dozen of them, with their kids leaping beside them, and a long-bearded billy-goat bringing up the rear.

And last it was 'Count for horses'. And did she nearly burst herself? She did, but she managed to count to thirty; and the thirty horses that came galloping out of the lake in their fives were such as the shepherd had never seen on earth: shining grey like twilit water, with gleams of brightness on them, and manes like white water-falls, and white tails that swept the ground.

'I have brought you a dowry worth having!' said the maiden.

All these animals she and the shepherd drove to his home. And as soon as ever might be, they were married.

They prospered and lived for many years in great happiness. Three beautiful boys were born to them. There was something special about these boys, as well there might be, having such a mother, and such a grandfather—not to speak of their grandmother on their father's side, who was a clever old body in her matter of fact way, and kept the balance in them between magic and common sense.

It seemed to the shepherd that his wife never grew any older; and she remained as beautiful as she had ever been. He couldn't do enough for her; and she was gentle and kind and thanked him for all he did.

But one day he saw her looking troubled, and he said, 'Tell me your trouble that I may lighten it.'

'I am remembering my father's words,' said she, 'about earth and iron. But you will never strike me, my husband, will you?'

'Strike you!' cried he. 'I would sooner lose my life!'

So then she smiled; but all the same, the smile was just a little sad.

Of all the food they ate together, she liked best bread and apples, for neither of these had she tasted before she came out of the water. The shepherd's mother baked the bread; but the apples he bought from a neighbour's orchard. And then he thought, 'If my wife likes apples so much, we ought to have a tree of our own; then she could pick an apple whenever she fancied.'

So he went to his neighbour and bought a little apple tree.

He came back very proudly.

'I have a surprise for you, my wife,' he said. And he showed her the apple tree.

She clapped her hands and said, 'Let us go and plant it together!'

He took a spade, and they went to a corner of the garden. He dug a deep hole, and his wife said, 'Now I will hold the tree straight, and you shall fill in the earth.'

But when they put the tree in the hole and spread out its roots, they found that the hole was not quite wide enough. So the shepherd began to dig it larger. He took out one spadeful of earth; he took out two spadefuls of earth.

'One more spadeful out, and it will do!' said she.

Alas! Alas! What was the shepherd thinking of? He spat on his hands, stooped low, filled the spade full, full, and flung the earth, with never a look where it was going, over his shoulder, right into the breast of his wife.

She dropped the tree and gave a wailing cry. He dropped the spade and took her in his arms. 'Have I hurt you, my wife? Oh say, say that I have not hurt you!'

'You have struck me with earth,' she said, very low, very frightened.

'But not with iron!' he cried.

'No, not with iron—yet,' said she. 'But the first part of the marriage bond is broken.'

'We will not keep the accursed tree!' said he. 'It shall go back whence it came!'

He went for a bridle to catch a horse and ride back to his neighbour's with the tree. And his wife went with him into the fields where the horses grazed. But not one of them would be caught. They galloped about the field, tossing their heads and waving their long white tails, as if they knew something bad would happen. But at last the shepherd and his wife managed to drive one horse into a corner, and they came up stealthily, one on each side of it.

The shepherd had the bridle in his hand. He was just about to slip it over the horse's head when the horse jerked his head aside, the bridle flew from the shepherd's hand, and the iron bit struck his wife on the cheek.

Then such a cry rang from her lips as none had ever heard before.

'First with earth, and then with iron! Farewell, my husband! Farewell forever!'

And she turned from him and fled, faster than any wind blows, towards the lake.

The shepherd rushed after her. But when he reached the lake, she was already far, far out, gliding along the surface of the water. And when she reached the middle of the lake, she stood there on the water, and called out:

'Bridle cow, white speckled,
Spotted cow, bold freckled.
Old white face, and grey Geringer,
And the white bull from the king's coast,
Grey ox and black calf,
Cow, calf, bull, and heifer,
All, all follow me home!'

Then from the meadows came the sound of trampling hoofs, and the shepherd, looking round, saw all his herd of cattle bearing down upon the lake. Not once did they pause. They came to the lake, and plunged in. The little black calf had been slaughtered, and was hanging from a hook; but it got off the hook alive and well, and trotted after the others down to the lake. Four oxen had been ploughing; they left the furrows and came, dragging the plough with them down into the water.

And still the wife stood on the water and called. She called the sheep, she called the goats, and last she called the horses: there they came, the sheep trotting, the goats leaping, the horses galloping. Only when the last of the flocks and herds had vanished under the water did the wife cease calling. Then she stretched out her arms to the shepherd, and with a last cry, 'Farewell! Farewell!' she too disappeared under the water.

For many and many a long weary day did the shepherd and his three sons wander by the shores of the lake, but never a glimpse did they get again of the one they sought. Years passed. The shepherd's old mother died. More years passed: the shepherd, too, went to his rest. Now only the three sons were left.

And then, on a grey day in autumn, as those three sons stood by the lake, they saw the waters stir, and their mother rose out of the waters and came to them. In her magic hands she brought them the gift of healing; and they all three became great physicians, mightier in their healing powers than any known in the country either before their day, or after it.

16

The Four Abdallahs

Once upon a time, in an eastern country, there lived a fisherman called Abdallah. He had a wife and nine sons, and he had a fishing net; but that was all he had. Every day he went fishing. When he caught but little, he sold that little and bought bread. When he caught much, he sold some, and kept some, and the family had fish for dinner. But they were very poor.

Now there came a day when his wife had yet another baby. And Abdallah said, 'I will go fishing today for the luck of the new-born.' But all that day he fished, and caught nothing.

So in the evening he turned to go home, very miserable. And going through the town he came to a baker's shop. The smell of the newly baked bread filled the air, making Abdallah's mouth water. He was hurrying by the shop, trying not to think of his own hunger, or of the hungry little ones at home, when the baker called to him, 'Come hither, oh fisherman!'

Abdallah went to stand before the baker. But when the baker said, 'Do you want bread?' Abdallah was silent.

'Do not be ashamed to speak,' said the baker. 'If you have no money I will give you bread and wait for my payment.'

'Indeed, master, I have no money,' said Abdallah; 'but if you will give me bread for my family, I will leave this net in pawn.'

'Nay, nay,' said the baker. 'The net is as it were your shop. If you give it in pawn, with what will you fish? Tell me how much bread you need.'

'Ten loaves,' said Abdallah.

Then the baker gave Abdallah ten loaves; and he gave him also ten coins to buy meat for his family.

'Now,' said he, 'you owe me twenty coins. When you have a good catch, you can repay me the value in fish.'

Abdallah thanked the baker with tears in his eyes, and went to spend the ten coins on meat and fruit. Then he hurried home to find the children crying with hunger. But they all had a good meal, and after that they were laughing, not crying.

Next day, Abdallah went to fish again. He fished all day, and again he caught nothing. On his way home he tried to hurry past the baker's shop. But the baker called to him and said, 'Brother, brother! Receive your bread and your money!'

And he again gave Abdallah the ten loaves and the ten coins.

So it went on for forty days. Abdallah fished, and caught nothing.

And every day, on his way home, he tried to hurry past the baker's shop; but every day the baker called to him and gave him the ten loaves and the ten coins. And when Abdallah said, 'Brother, the reckoning grows very heavy,' the baker answered, 'This is not the time for reckoning. Wait for your good fortune, then I will reckon with you.'

Abdallah felt ashamed and said to his wife, 'I will cut up this net and go fishing no more.' But his wife said, 'Go and fish in a new place, and maybe your luck will turn.'

So Abdallah went to a place farther along the shore and cast in his net. And immediately something stirred in the net; and the net was so heavy that Abdallah could scarcely draw it out of the water. But he strained and tugged, and at last he got that net ashore, and looked to see what was in it. And then he gave a great cry and fled away; for looking up at him through the meshes of the net was the face of a merman.

'Come back, come back!' cried the merman. 'I won't hurt you! I was but going about my business; and indeed I was as frightened as you are, when the net closed over me. I could have torn your net to pieces, but you see I did not. Come, release me, and let us be friends!'

So Abdallah came back and lifted the net from off the merman; and the merman went back into the shallows and sat on a rock. He put his head up above the water and said, 'What is your name?'

'Abdallah.'

'That is my name also,' said the merman. 'I am Abdallah of the Sea, and you are Abdallah of the Land. On the land you have fruits— grapes, figs, water melons, peaches, and pomegranates. In the sea we have jewels—pearls and diamonds, rubies, sapphires and emeralds.

Let us now, as friends, exchange the fruits of the land for the fruits of the sea. If every day, at sunrising, you will come to this place with a basket of fruits, and call out, "Where are you, Abdallah, you of the Sea?" I shall hear and come, and receive the fruits, and in return fill your basket with jewels. But wait now, and I will bring you a present.' Then the merman swam away.

'He is gone,' thought Abdallah. 'I have been a fool. I ought to have kept him in the net. I could at least have shown him in the town, and earned some coins to repay the baker.'

He took up his net and was starting for home, when the merman came back again with his two hands full of jewels.

'I have no basket,' he said, 'or I would have filled it. But take these now, and come again tomorrow, bringing me fruits in a basket. And I will fill the basket with jewels. And so it shall be every day between us. We will both keep faith.'

Abdallah of the Land took his jewels joyfully from Abdallah of the Sea, and hurried to the baker.

'Oh my brother, my brother, good fortune has befallen us!'

And he gave the baker one handful of jewels.

'Now my debt is paid,' said he. 'But lend me a little money to spend today, until I can sell the rest of these jewels.'

The baker opened his money chest, and gave Abdallah every coin that was in it. And he filled a basket with bread, and put the basket on his head, and walked behind Abdallah to his house. And then he went to the market, and bought meat and fruit and vegetables, and came again to Abdallah's house carrying these things.

'My friend, you have wearied yourself,' said Abdallah.

But the baker said, 'This I must do. Your generosity has overwhelmed me, and I have become your servant.'

And Abdallah answered, 'Remember who gave to me in the time of my distress.'

So they rejoiced and made merry; and the baker spent the evening feasting with Abdallah and his family.

Next morning, Abdallah filled a basket with fruit, and went to the shore and called, 'Where are you, Abdallah, you of the Sea?' And the merman came and took the basket and swam off with it; and very soon returned with the basket filled with jewels.

Abdallah set off home with the basket, and when he came to the baker's shop, the baker called to him, and said, 'Oh my master, I have baked forty buns for you.'

But Abdallah said, 'Do not call me "master"!' And he gave the baker three handfuls of jewels. Then he went to the jewel market, and sought out the sheik of the market, and showed him the basket, and said, 'I wish to sell these jewels. What will you give me?'

The sheik turned and shouted to his officers, 'Lay hold of this man and bind him fast! This is the thief who stole the queen's necklace!'

And the officers ran up and bound Abdallah's hands behind his back, and drove him with whips to the king's palace. And all the jewel sellers in the market followed after him, crying out, 'The thief! The thief! We have caught the man who stole the queen's jewels!'

So they brought Abdallah before the king, and the sheik said, 'Oh king, when the queen's necklace was stolen, you bade us look out for the thief. Lo, here he is, and here are the jewels!'

The king said, 'These do not look like the queen's jewels; but we will send them to her and see.'

So a servant took the jewels to the queen, and came back with a message. The queen said, 'I have found my necklace, and these jewels are not mine—they are far finer. If the owner will sell, buy them for your little daughter.'

The king turned angrily to the sheik and said, 'What have you done? You have bound and beaten an innocent man!'

The sheik grovelled before the king and answered, 'Oh my king, we knew that he was a poor man. How came he to possess such jewels if he had not stolen them?'

And the king said, 'Why didn't you ask him? Get out of my sight— you and your company! May God not bless you!'

So the sheik of the market and the jewel sellers went sadly away, and the king turned to Abdallah. 'All this time you have not opened your mouth. But now, tell me truly, where did you get these priceless things?' So Abdallah told the king the whole story.

And the king said, 'Brother, Heaven has blessed you! But wealth must not appear in dirt and rags.' And he ordered his servants to take Abdallah to the bath, and clothe him in splendid garments. And when Abdallah came back, bathed and scented and dressed like a lord, the king said, 'Now you appear as befits your station, and I will make you my vizier. Are you a single man, or have you a wife?'

'I have a wife and ten children.'

The king summoned the great ladies of the court, and his couriers and his officers of the guard, and sent them to Abdallah's house to fetch his wife and the children. The great ladies clothed her in garments like their own, and her children in fine garments also. Then they set her and the children in a litter, and the couriers and the officers of the guard marched before her, and Abdallah's wife arrived at the palace seated in the litter, with her little baby in her arms and her nine boys clustered about her.

The king gave them a wing in the palace to live in, and he had the nine boys brought before him. He was delighted with the boys, because he had no sons, but only one little daughter. So he betrothed the eldest son to his daughter; and they held a betrothal feast, and Abdallah sat at the king's right hand.

The next day, at sunrising, the king looked out of his window and saw Abdallah walking away with a basket of fruit on his head. So he called out, 'Abdallah, where are you going?'

'To my companion, Abdallah of the Sea.'

The king said, 'This is not the moment to go!'

But Abdallah answered, 'I fear to be unfaithful to him. He will say that worldly matters have hardened my heart.'

And the king said, 'You speak truly. Go to your companion.'

So Abdallah went down to the shore and called, 'Where are you, Abdallah, you of the Sea?' And Abdallah of the Sea came, and they exchanged fruits for jewels.

They did this every day; and every day as Abdallah came back through the town with his basket of jewels, he passed by the baker's shop; but always he found it closed. So, after ten days, he spoke to the man who lived next door to the shop and asked, 'Where is the baker?'

'He is at home, and he is very ill,' said the man.

'And where is his house?' So the man told him, and Abdallah went to the baker's house and knocked.

And when he had knocked many times, the baker put his head out of the window; and seeing Abdallah, he came down and opened the door, and drew him inside quickly, and embraced him.

'They told me you were very ill,' said Abdallah. 'But I find you well!'

'No, I am not ill,' said the baker. 'But I heard you had been taken for a thief, and I was afraid, and hid myself.'

So then Abdallah told the baker that he was now the king's vizier. And he gave the baker all the jewels he had with him, and went back to the palace with an empty basket.

When the king saw the empty basket, he said, 'You have not met your companion today?'

'Yes, I met him. And as usual he filled my basket. But I have given all the jewels to the baker.'

The king said, 'Who is this baker?'

So Abdallah told the king that it was the baker who had befriended him when he was without food and without money.

Said the king, 'What is his name?'

And Abdallah answered, 'He is Abdallah the Baker. I am Abdallah of the Land, and my other friend is Abdallah of the Sea.'

Said the king, 'Fate plays a hand in this! My name also is Abdallah. Abd-Allah means "servant of God", and all servants of God are brothers. Go, bring the baker. I will make him Vizier of the Left, and you shall be Vizier of the Right.'

So Abdallah of the Land fetched Abdallah the Baker, and Abdallah the King had him clothed splendidly, and made him Vizier of the Left. He stood behind the throne at the king's left hand; and Abdallah of the Land stood behind the throne at the king's right hand.

And at sunrising on each new day Abdallah of the Land carried his basket of fruits down to Abdallah of the Sea, and returned with the basket filled with jewels. All these jewels he shared with Abdallah the King and Abdallah the Baker; so that there were no richer men than those Abdallahs anywhere in the world.

CPSIA information can be obtained
at www.ICGtesting.com
Printed in the USA
FSOW01n0218040416
18703FS

9 780997 294712